SURFING THE HIMALAYAS

Surfing the Himalayas

Conversations and Travels
With Master Fwap

Rama – Dr Frederick Lenz

Hodder & Stoughton
LONDON SYDNEY AUCKLAND

Copyright © Rama – Dr Frederick Lenz 1994

The right of Rama – Dr Frederick Lenz to be identified as the
Author of this work has been asserted by him in accordance with
the Copyright, Designs and Patents Act 1988.

First published in Great Britain in 1995 by Hodder and
Stoughton
A division of Hodder Headline PLC

10 9 8 7 6 5 4 3 2 1

A CIP catalogue record for this title is available from the
British Library

ISBN 0 340 65799 5

Typeset by Palimpsest Book Production Limited,
Polmont, Stirlingshire
Printed and bound in Great Britain by
Cox & Wyman Ltd, Reading, Berkshire

Hodder and Stoughton
A division of Hodder Headline PLC
338 Euston Road
London NW1 3BH

This book of my Himalayan Adventures is dedicated to
those who seek Enlightenment and Laughter

ॐ

The following account of my Himalayan adventures is based upon a series of experiences that occurred to me some time ago in Nepal. I have taken the liberty of transforming these accounts, even though they are based on real life occurrences, into a work of fiction. I hope that the internal and external experiences presented in the following pages both entertain and enlighten you.

Rama – Dr Frederick Lenz

ॐ

ༀ་མ་ཎི་པ་དྨེ་ཧཱུྃ

CHAPTER ONE

Journey to Nepal

ॐ

I have always been in love with the snow. There is something about its perfect crystal whiteness that transports me to happiness. On frozen blizzard nights, when sensible men and women stay safely indoors by their cozy fireplaces, while their children sleep snug as bugs in a rug in warm beds, covered by blankets and fluffy down comforters, I walk alone in the wind-whipped snow, down lonely pine-trimmed lanes.

My fascination with snow began when I was a child. On cold winter mornings and frozen afternoons I played in the snow until, red-cheeked and frozen-fingered, I was called indoors by my mother. She handed me hot chocolate and then dried my soaking clothes, boots and gloves by the fireplace.

As soon as my clothes were dry and I had slipped them back on, I ran outside again to the snowy whiteness in our backyard, where I played happily until the sun set, and the first stars of evening began to appear.

ॐ

I probably would have grown up to be a doctor (as my mother wished), or gone on to law school and become an attorney (as my father advised) if, on my seventh birthday, my grandparents hadn't given me my first sled.

It was a bleached oak Flexible Flyer with fire engine red steel runners. The words 'Flexible Flyer' were proudly stencilled in big black letters, for all the world to see, across the top of its blond oak body. I spent the better part of that winter – and many winters that followed – on top of my Flexible Flyer, rapidly rushing down every steep snow-covered slope I could find.

There's nothing like gliding on snow. The cold wind rushes up to greet your face as you careen madly down a sharp slope. You steer with your hands and hope to gain extra speed by pressing your body as flatly as possible against your sled. Maneuvering quickly, first left and then right, I always aimed for the steepest downhill sections of the trail to gain maximum velocity.

I spent many freeze-dried winter afternoons perfecting my maneuvers for taking corners faster. As soon as I reached the bottom of a hill, I would immediately rush back up to the top again, laughing and dragging my sled behind me. Once there, without pausing to catch my breath, I would dive back on top of my sled and tear down the hillside again. Eventually I could sled down a slope faster than any of my friends could.

It was logical, I suppose, that as I grew older I would graduate from sledding to snowboarding. Skiing was too social a sport for me: it lacked the pure intensity and grace of standing on top of a four-and-a-half-foot-long fiberglass board while plummeting straight down mountains of snow.

Having successfully snowboarded most of the higher mountains in the United States and Canada, I packed my bags and two snowboards, said good-bye to my friends and relations, and travelled by plane to Nepal, to snowsurf the Himalayas on the roof of the world.

I flew with the Baron on Lufthansa to Frankfurt, where I changed planes for Katmandu. I arrived late on a cold January afternoon and, after clearing Nepalese customs, I went straight to the Katmandu Youth Hostel.

The hostel was located on the eastern side of Katmandu. It was a two-story brick and stucco building with very small windows. Inside, there were cots and lots of European college students. Most of them had come to Nepal looking for 'enlightenment,' which they hoped to find while seated at the feet of a local Buddhist monk.

The food that was served at the hostel was simple but good. There were two hot soups, doughy pan bread and tea. After checking in, I ate and chatted with a blonde German college girl who was also staying there. Seeing my snowboards leaning against the wall she proceeded to ask me, in her heavily accented English phrases, lots of questions about snowboarding.

I answered her questions for about an hour, and then, yawning with fatigue, I excused myself. After washing with freezing cold water – since no hot water was left – I crawled into my sleeping bag, fell asleep, and had a most unusual dream.

3

In my dream, I was snowboarding down a gigantic mountain. The slope below me went straight down as far as I could see. I was riding on my snowboard, happily cutting in and out of the deep granular powder, when suddenly, from out of nowhere, a small, bald-headed Buddhist monk, dressed in a saffron-colored robe, appeared right in front of me!

I reflexively cut my snowboard left to avoid hitting him, but he remained in front of me! Then I tried cutting right to avoid him, but he was still there! It didn't seem to make any difference which way or how I maneuvered my snowboard; he always managed to stay several feet ahead of me!

Accepting the fact that I couldn't get away from him – for some reason it is easy to accept the most extraordinary situations as ordinary in dreams – I found myself staring at the short, bald-headed Buddhist monk.

A soft, beautiful, golden phosphorescent light emanated from and surrounded his entire body. As I examined him more closely, I found my gaze irresistibly drawn to his face, which was creased and wrinkled with many fine lines of age.

As I stared at him, the bald-headed monk looked back impassively at me. Then, quite unexpectedly, he winked. He then disappeared as quickly as he had appeared!

Looking ahead, I saw that I was rapidly snowboarding toward the edge of a cliff. Before I could stop myself, I shot over the cliff's edge and – in a nightmarish turn of events – I found myself plummeting straight down into an endless chasm of snow!

I was about to start yelling when I heard a voice coming from my right side. In a firm male tone, it said: 'Don't give up. Fly! Use your mind. You can do it!'

Glancing quickly to my right, I saw that the short, bald-headed monk had suddenly reappeared. He was standing in the air right next to me, and was falling at precisely the same rate of speed that I was.

'Fly! Just do it!' he said to me even more firmly. 'What other choice do you have? Use your willpower. Do it now or you will die and never get to meet and help all the people that you are supposed to!'

Listening to him speak, I somehow suddenly knew just what to do: By pushing down with my feelings, I began to gradually slow my descent. By pushing down harder with my feelings, I was able to stop myself in midair. By pushing down as hard as I could, I began to slowly ascend. Using my feelings to propel and direct myself, I flew upward through the air on my snowboard, until I reached the safety of the cliff above. Then I stopped.

'Now that wasn't so hard, was it?' I heard the same voice ask me.

I looked around for the bald-headed monk, but he was nowhere in sight. His ability to rapidly appear and disappear, and to speak without being seen, was beginning to annoy me.

'Don't worry about where I am,' he said. 'You will see me soon enough.'

And with his words still echoing in my mind, I was awakened by the sun shining through the youth hostel windows onto my face, to my first morning in Nepal.

ॐ

After washing and dressing, I had a quick breakfast of hot tea and cold pan bread dipped in honey. Then I headed outside to explore Katmandu. The narrow, early morning streets were already filled with people shopping for food and other goods.

I walked happily through the crowds, listening to the singsong sounds of the Nepalese shopkeepers selling their wares. As I strolled along the city streets, the pungent smells of saffron, cumin, and coriander emanated from the restaurants and spice stalls, perfuming the morning air.

I had entirely forgotten about my dream from the night before until I saw several bald-headed Buddhist monks, dressed in their brightly colored ochre robes, walking toward me on the street. Seeing them reawakened the memory of the levitating monk I had dreamt about the night before.

As I watched the monks walking toward me, I had the crazy notion that if I were able to focus my will hard enough – as I had in my dream the previous night – I would be able to fly up into the sky and hover above their heads! I laughed silently at the absurdity of my thoughts, and at that exact moment the approaching monks grinned openly and widely at me. I couldn't help but wonder, as they strolled past me, if they had somehow telepathically read my thoughts, and if they were as amused by them as I was.

After walking through the streets of the city for about an hour, I began to approach the outskirts of Katmandu. It was there that I had my first real glimpse of the Himalayas. The giant, snow-covered mountains rose from the distant horizon and disappeared from sight into the white and gray clouds that constantly hovered above them. Daylight and the shadows cast by moving clouds played back and forth upon their glistening slopes.

I stared at the Himalayas for what seemed like an endless time. Their effect upon me was immediate and magnetic: I knew right there and then that the time had come for me to surf the Himalayas!

The Nepalese receptionist at the Katmandu Youth Hostel arranged for me to get a ride up to the mountains with a local farmer, in the back of his yak-drawn cart. Sitting in his cart, on a pile of straw, next to my snowboard, I listened to the driver's non-stop comments without understanding a word he said.

Every time we passed a temple or a large building, he raised his right arm and pointed to it. Then he smiled at me, and in an excited voice, said something in Nepali that I couldn't understand. In an attempt to be polite, I smiled back at him and nodded my head affirmatively – as if I understood what he had just said – as we bumped and bounced along the rock and gravel road together.

After we had ridden in his cart together for several hours, the road turned sharply upward and I began to get a closer look at the Himalayas. I was totally transfixed by their rough and jagged beauty. Staring at them from the back of the cart, I had a sudden experience of déjà vu. I clearly sensed that in some way, and at some other time, I had been in these majestic mountains before, even though this was the first time in my life I had ever visited the Himalayas.

We gradually made our way up a high mountain pass. When we reached the crest of the pass, I motioned to the driver to stop and let me off; a small path wound its way skyward from that point to a higher section of the mountain than the road serviced. To get to the top of the mountain, I would have to proceed the rest of the way on foot.

After I had taken my snowboard and the rest of my gear out of his cart, I thanked the driver in English and waved. He smiled and waved back at me. Then he said something to me in Nepali as he pointed up to the top of the mountain. I thought I detected a tone of warning in his voice, but for all I knew he was wishing me good luck!

Turning around and waving good-bye to me, he drove off in his cart, leaving me alone, in the late afternoon snow, halfway up my first Himalayan mountain. Strapping my board and day pack onto my back, I began the long, slow, and arduous climb up the steep and rocky trail that led to the mountain's summit.

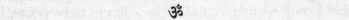

CHAPTER TWO

How I Met Master Fwap

ॐ

After climbing steadily up the steep trail for more than three hours, I finally reached the mountain's summit. Unlike the mountains in the United States that I was used to snowboarding, the Himalayas had no chair lifts or rapid trams to ride up to the tops of the mountains. Standing on the crest of my first Himalayan mountain, drenched in perspiration from my ascent, I looked down over the snow-covered slopes below me.

As I gazed out over the distant horizon, I suddenly realized that I was on top of a mountain that was twice as high as any I had ever snowboarded before. Standing there, listening to the sound of the wind, I secretly hoped that the mountain I was on was not particularly prone to avalanches.

I had brought the longer of my two snowboards with me that day. While slightly less maneuverable than my short board, my long board was faster and better suited to deep powder.

After removing my day pack from my back, I unzipped it and pulled out my snowboarding boots. Then I rapidly unlaced and took off my hiking boots. After slipping on my snowboarding boots, I placed my hiking boots back inside my day pack, zipped it back up and reshouldered it. Finally, I placed my goggles over my eyes, mounted my snowboard and prepared to snowsurf down my first Himalayan peak.

The ride down was fantastic! I shot through the deep powder like a bullet. Near the end of my run, the terrain began to flatten out and I started to slow down. It was right then and there that I surfed my first Buddhist monk!

He seemed to have come from nowhere. At first I thought I was dreaming again. But there, not twenty feet in front of my rapidly descending snowboard, stood a short Buddhist monk in a saffron-colored robe!

Unlike the monk that had been in my dream the night before, however, the monk that was now standing right in front of my rapidly descending snowboard did not magically keep the same distance ahead of me. Instead, even though I cut left, hard and fast, to avoid hitting him, I plowed right into him! The force of our collision sent the two of us tumbling onto the snow-covered ground.

Fortunately for the bald-headed monk, I wasn't moving very fast when I snowboarded him. Unfortunately for me, after we had both stopped rolling in the snow and gotten back up onto our feet again, it was more than evident from the expression on the monk's face that he was really pissed off!

I walked over to apologize to the bald-headed monk and to see if he was all right. While he clearly wasn't very happy with having just been snowboarded, he otherwise seemed fine. I glanced at his face, and much to my surprise, I recognized him. He was the same bald-headed monk that I had seen in my dream the night before!

I stared at him silently, not knowing what to say or how to say it. I suddenly wished that I had taken a crash course in Nepali just prior to hitting him. After several more moments had passed, I broke the uncomfortable silence that was rapidly settling in between us. Even though I assumed he wouldn't understand a word I said to him, I apologized in English to the short, bald-headed monk, who was still brushing snow from his robe. I felt an apology of some kind, even if it was in the wrong language, would be better than no apology at all.

Judging from the intensity of the expression on his face, he seemed to be listening very seriously to what I was saying to him. After I finished my apology, his face seemed to relax, and he no longer looked quite as upset.

I wanted to tell the bald-headed monk about seeing him in my dream, but in addition to my inability to speak Nepali, somehow it didn't seem like quite the right moment to strike up a casual conversation with him.

Several more moments of silence passed as we both stared at each other. Then the short, bald-headed monk, whose face was still covered with flecks of snow from his recent close encounter with a snowboarding American young adult, spoke to me – not in the singsong Nepali that I would have expected from him, but in perfectly graceful, although slightly accented English.

'Our meeting was fated and your karma caused it to happen,' he began. 'An apology for what was inevitable is totally unnecessary. Also, as you can see for yourself, I am unhurt. You look like you took much more of a tumble than I did, young man.'

'I saw you in a dream I had last night!' I blurted out.

'That was not a dream,' he replied. 'It was real.'

'But how can that be? Dreams aren't real, are they?' I asked.

'Oh but they are, my young friend, they are! Come, come! Get the board that you flew down from the mountain on and walk with me back to Katmandu. We will talk as we walk. Come now – we must hurry along. The sun will soon be setting, and then it will be too cold out here even for one of Buddha's monks!'

As he spoke, I thought of the long walk that lay ahead of me back to the hostel in Katmandu, and suddenly I realized that I was extremely tired. As if he had been reading my mind, the bald-headed monk said, 'I am sure we will not have to walk too far along this road before someone who is driving to Katmandu will come along and give us a lift. There are certain advantages, my young friend, to being one of Buddha's monks!'

He smiled at me and proceeded to introduce himself. 'My name is Master Fwap Sam-Dup. I am the last master of the Rae Chorze-Fwaz School of Tantric Mysticism and Buddhist Enlightenment. You can call me Master Fwap if you like.'

After introducing himself, he quickly and gracefully bowed to me. He then asked me what my name was.

I introduced myself to the aged monk, after which I bowed back to him, awkwardly and self-consciously. His eyes twinkled as he watched me, and I could tell he was secretly amused by the complete lack of *savoir faire* that I exhibited in my bow to him.

Exchanging my snowboarding boots for my hiking boots, I shouldered my day pack and strapped my long board onto my back. Then the two of us walked down the remainder of the snow-covered mountain slope, until we reached the gravel road below.

How I Met Master Fwap

CHAPTER THREE

The Road to Katmandu

ॐ

We walked down the rest of the slope without speaking.
The only audible sound was the continuous crunch-
crunch-crunching of my hiking boots on the frozen
snow. When we finally reached the road I had to sit down
and rest for a few minutes; I was both physically and
mentally exhausted from the altitude, the excitement of
having just snowboarded my first Himalayan mountain,
and the incredulity of walking down a mountain next to
a short, bald-headed Buddhist monk, whom I had met
the night before in a dream, and surfed today!

While I was sitting on the snow-covered ground,
trying as best I could to pull myself together, Master
Fwap began to softly sing a Buddhist chant. The sound
of his voice soothed me. After listening to him sing for
a few minutes, I felt refreshed and relaxed. I stood up,
and then Master Fwap and I began walking down the
road to Katmandu together.

While I was walking along the road next to Master
Fwap, I had the opportunity to examine him more
closely. He was approximately five-feet, two inches

tall. He was very thin; he couldn't have weighed more than one hundred and twenty-five pounds. From my six-foot-three-inch vantage point, I had an excellent view of his neatly shaved round head.

His face, like so many of the Nepalese people, was gently wrinkled from a lifetime of exposure to bright sunlight and extreme high altitude. But even though his skin was marked with many small fine lines of age, it didn't seem old and worn. In fact, his skin had a healthy and youthful glow.

I guessed that Master Fwap was about seventy years old. His eyes were hazel-colored, although they seemed to change hue according to his mood. When he smiled – which was quite frequently – he revealed a perfect set of pearly white teeth.

His saffron-colored monk's robe looked ancient. In places, its color was uneven and faded from extended exposure to the sun. He wore small boots with high stockings and walked with a graceful agility. I had some difficulty keeping up with him as we walked along the road to Katmandu together.

It was his eyes that kept catching my attention as we walked. They sparkled with an inner power and intelligence I had never witnessed in anyone else before. Walking next to Master Fwap, I had the strange and haunting feeling that I had always known him. For some unknown reason, it didn't seem to be at all unusual or out of place for the two of us to be out walking together in the winter snow, down a Himalayan road, on a late January afternoon.

'I sensed that we would be bumping into each other soon,' he laughed, 'although I must admit I didn't know that today would be the day. My own master, Fwaz Shastra-Dup, foretold of our meeting many long years ago. He said that one day I would run into a tall Western youth on this very mountain. I must admit though, at the time, I didn't take his comments quite this literally!' he said with a hearty laugh.

'If you don't mind,' he continued, 'I will tell you a little bit about myself as we walk. Then tomorrow, if you like, you can come to the temple where I live and visit me. It is on the western side of Katmandu, on the outskirts of town, in the foothills.'

As we walked along the road to Katmandu, Master Fwap began to tell me about his life. He said that he had been born in a small village in eastern Tibet. As a child he had shown an early aptitude for Buddhism, and so – as was the custom in Tibet at that time – on his tenth birthday his parents admitted him to the local monastery to study Buddhist Yoga and to become a monk.

Master Fwap told me he had spent many happy years growing up in the monastery. The senior monks taught him the Buddhist scriptures, meditation, astrology and Tibetan medicine, while he practiced Buddhist debate and martial arts with some of the younger monks.

Master Fwap said that although the senior monks who taught and resided in his monastery were very knowledgeable about meditation and Buddhist Yoga, unfortunately none of them were 'enlightened.' At the age of nineteen, when he had learned all he felt he could from the senior monks, he decided to leave the monastery and search for an enlightened Buddhist master of his own. Master Fwap explained to me that to become enlightened, it was necessary to first find and study with an enlightened Buddhist master.

'I knew that only a fully enlightened Buddhist Yoga master, who had the full power of enlightenment at his disposal,' Master Fwap explained, 'would be able to show me how to attain enlightenment and reach nirvana in this very lifetime.'

In his search for a fully enlightened master of his own, the young Master Fwap travelled and roamed for many years throughout Tibet, Nepal, Bhutan, Sikkim, China and India. In his travels he had met many Buddhist Yoga masters, some of whom could perform miracles!

I asked Master Fwap if he would tell me about some of the miracles he had seen the Buddhist masters perform. He told me he had met Buddhist masters who could levitate, heal the sick, become invisible at will, fill the night sky with white and colored light, open interdimensional doorways, and do many other incredible things. He said the unusual powers these masters possessed that enabled them to perform these miracles were called 'siddhas.' He explained that the masters he had met gained their siddha powers from many years of meditation upon their 'chakras.'

At that point, I interrupted Master Fwap's narration and asked him if he would explain to me what chakras were. He told me that chakras are mystical energy centers that exist within the human aura. He said every living being has an aura, a field of psychic energy that surrounds and protects its physical body from negative psychic energies. He explained that the aura is the body's 'psychic immune system.'

Master Fwap further explained that tremendous occult power resides in a person's chakras, and that siddha masters draw upon that power during their meditation practices, store it within themselves, and later use it to perform miracles.

18

From a Buddhist point of view, Master Fwap said, having siddha powers and being a siddha master was indeed a great yogic accomplishment, but it was not the same as being enlightened. He remarked that many people commonly confuse siddha masters, who have the power to perform miracles through the activation of their chakras, with enlightened masters, who can enter into a deep meditative state of emptiness (which he referred to as 'samadhi').

Master Fwap told me that, while he had been very impressed by the siddha masters he had met, by the powers they wielded and by the miracles that they could perform, he hadn't really felt that any of them were truly 'enlightened.'

I then asked Master Fwap – after first admitting to him that I had absolutely no idea what enlightenment was, or why anyone would want to seek it – how he could tell if a Buddhist master was really 'enlightened' in the first place.

Master Fwap responded that, in his opinion, there were two conditions that would indicate whether or not a Buddhist master was truly enlightened. The first condition was that the master's aura would turn a beautiful bright golden color when he meditated.

'Do you mean to say that you can actually see golden light surrounding an enlightened master's body, Master Fwap?' I asked him with some incredulity.

'Oh yes, most definitely!' he said, as he nodded his head in affirmation. 'Almost anyone can see the golden light in an enlightened master's aura when the master meditates, unless, of course, the person is very blocked up psychically.'

Master Fwap elaborated, saying that sometimes you can see other colors in addition to gold in an enlightened master's aura, and at very special moments, you can simultaneously see many colors in a master's aura. He referred to this multicolored effect as a master's 'rainbow hue.'

Master Fwap went on to say that the second characteristic that would indicate whether or not a master was truly enlightened was his sense of humor. He remarked that an enlightened Buddhist master would always have a totally outrageous sense of humor, because life, when viewed through the eyes of enlightenment, was incredibly funny!

This surprised me. I guess I had always imagined somehow that Buddhist masters would be very stoical. Master Fwap informed me that while there are indeed as many sides to enlightenment as there are ways to achieve it, the experience of enlightenment always imparts a light and playful sense to both a master's teachings and personality.

Master Fwap went on to explain that sitting in front of an enlightened master while he is meditating is like being in the middle of an energy storm. 'At times,' he said, 'your entire body tingles with ecstasy as you feel the waves of psychic energy that emanate from the master's aura touching your own body.'

After his brief discussion about enlightenment, Master Fwap resumed his story about his search for an enlightened Buddhist master of his own. He told me that in all of his travels throughout the Orient, he had never encountered a master who fulfilled both of the necessary qualifications for enlightenment. He also said that while he had met a few very funny masters in his travels, none of them had emanated waves of golden light when they meditated.

ॐ

I asked Master Fwap if he had studied with any of the siddha masters he had met in his travels, and if so, had he learned how to do any miracles? To be honest, I was much more interested in hearing about the siddha masters and the miracles they performed than I was in learning about emptiness and enlightenment.

Master Fwap responded by saying that spiritual knowledge, which he called 'enlightened awareness,' is of much greater importance than the ability to perform a few miracles.

'Spiritual knowledge is the experience of enlightenment and requires an understanding of the innermost workings of the Enlightenment Cycle,' Master Fwap began.

'Spiritual knowledge is the awareness of the eternal side of things: the eternal side of ourselves, of others, and of the worlds that exist both within and outside of us.

'The attainment of enlightenment makes you happy forever!' he exclaimed joyously. 'It frees you from the mental and emotional pains that unenlightened human beings experience every day. When you are enlightened, you live in a condition of ecstasy, brightness and joy all of the time.

'The only reality that exists for most people,' Master Fwap continued, 'is the world that greets their physical eyes and other senses every day. They believe that *this* world,' he said, moving his arm in a large, sweeping gesture that encompassed the entire valley we were walking through, 'is all there is to life.

'The world that you see around you appears to be physical. It is filled with mountains, snow, plants, animals and people. It is ruled by time and the laws that govern matter and energy.

'It is a world in which we experience pleasure and

pain, loss and gain, birth and death, happiness and sorrow.

'Naturally, since most people are only aware of their physical natures and of the physical side of their lives, their happiness is extremely limited. When their physical lives are pleasant, when the events and circumstances in daily living turn out as they had wished or hoped, they will usually be happy for a short while. But when the events and circumstances in their lives don't turn out as they had hoped or wished, most often they experience a great deal of sorrow, unhappiness and pain.

'As I'm sure you know by now, based on your own experiences in life, most people aren't really very happy. Beyond their surface appearances – the smiles that they wear for the rest of the world to look at – most people are soulsick. The vast majority of people who populate our planet live lives of quiet desperation that are all too often quite harsh and painful – lives in which events and circumstances usually don't turn out the way they had hoped or planned.

'Most human beings are completely out of touch with their spiritual nature,' Master Fwap stated in a factual tone of voice, 'and with the inner dimensions that exist within themselves. They don't realize each person has a soul – an inner core of light and intelligence as vast as the ten thousand worlds – whose true nature is emptiness, ecstasy and happiness.'

'But Master Fwap!' I quickly interjected, 'Lots of people know they have a soul. They teach people about that in church.'

'Yes,' he replied. 'Some people do know they have a soul. But just because, at one time or another, a priest or a monk told them they have a soul, doesn't mean they have personally experienced their own soul, or know

22

how to get to it and bring its power, beauty, happiness and enlightenment into daily life.

'Human beings are soulsick because they are cut off from the ecstasy of creation! Enlightenment, which is the pure experience of the soul's light, is not simply an intellectual understanding one gains about living; it is a direct and powerful entrance into, and experience of, the most ancient, knowledgeable and eternal part of ourselves.

'We are luminous beings!' Master Fwap exclaimed. 'Beneath our transient physical bodies, we are made of intelligent light. One's own body of light – which I refer to as the soul – is the most real part of oneself because it lives forever. It doesn't die and decay along with the physical body after death. At the end of each of our lifetimes, it transmigrates – through the process of reincarnation – into a new body that is just in the process of being born. Then the soul begins the cycle of living all over again in a new incarnation!

'Beyond this world, the world we experience each day with our minds and our senses,' he continued, 'are countless other worlds and dimensions. In deep meditation, when your thoughts have become silent, and your emotions are calm and at peace, you can travel into and experience the inner worlds and dimensions of light and perfection, and even experience nirvana itself.

'There is no experience in this or any other world, whether it is in a physical or astral dimension, that can compare to the experience of enlightenment and nirvana. It is the highest ecstasy. There is nothing more.'

Master Fwap became silent. Talking about enlightenment and nirvana seemed to have transported him to another plane. Walking next to him, I had the peculiar feeling that he was not entirely in his body. He seemed to have gone far away, to a very private place that I couldn't quite see or reach.

After walking next to me in silence for several minutes, he began to speak again in a very quiet voice: 'The world that human beings have made for themselves is rampant with poverty, disease, famine and death. It is filled with war and war's alarms.

'Even when people manage, through luck, or through effort, to attain everything in life that they desire, their happiness is usually shallow and short-lived. Most successful people are surprised to find out that the attainment of their goals doesn't necessarily bring them the happiness and joy they assumed would accompany their successes. And even the lucky ones, who do manage to become happy by attaining their goals, live each day with the constant fear of losing whatever it is they may have gained.

'Even the rich aren't often happy. Their wealth is at best only a temporary distraction. It doesn't make them immune to emotional and mental suffering, or to disease and death. They too must deal with loneliness, the deaths of loved ones, and the frustrations and boredom of old age. The rich may have more material goods and benefits than the poor, but most often they tend to lead spiritually impoverished lives.

'Time holds the final claim check for everything we gain or attain in this lifetime!' Master Fwap stated emphatically. 'All of our possessions, along with the people and feelings we love, are at best only loaned to us for a very short time by eternity.

'If you live for a very long while, you will have to watch your friends and loved ones die, your body age and lose its beauty and vigor, and your mental capacities fade. All of your physical accomplishments, no matter how important and significant they might have seemed to you at one time, will be relegated to the past.

'At the end of your life you will probably end up in an old-age home, or in a back room in one of your children's houses, left only with a handful of fading memories and a body racked with great pain and suffering.

'Unless you have gained the happiness and ecstasy that comes from the practice of meditation, the inevitable destruction of everything that you have loved and worked for will cause you to be very sad and lonely during the final days of your life here on this earth.'

'But Master Fwap, how can enlightenment change any of that?' I asked. 'Just because you are enlightened doesn't mean you aren't going to die, or that you will be protected from bad experiences in life, does it?'

Master Fwap smiled at me and laughed. 'No,' he said, 'enlightenment won't enable you to live forever in your current physical body, nor will it prevent all physical misfortunes from befalling you – although it will certainly help you avoid a great many of them,' he replied.

'Then what good is it?' I asked.

'Enlightenment makes you happy!' Master Fwap responded with a broad smile. 'It is the experience of ecstasy beyond anything you can possibly imagine. Knowledge of the Enlightenment Cycle – of the ways that the inner dimensions and nirvana work – gives you an entirely new perspective on everything. It lifts you far above the transient sorrows, pains, pleasures and joys that the unenlightened masses experience each and every day of their lives.'

ॐ

Master Fwap Explains Enlightenment

It was getting colder and so far no cars or trucks had passed us. I zipped my down parka up all the way. After walking down the road for a few more minutes, I broke the silence that had settled in between us; I asked Master Fwap if he could give me a 'brief' definition of enlightenment. He laughed so hard that his whole body shook. Then, to the best of my recollection, this is what he said.

'Enlightenment is the complete awareness of life, without any mental modifications. It is the experience of everything – every dimensional plane, world and reality. It occurs when your mind merges with nirvana, with what we Tibetans call the Dharma-Käya – the clear light of reality – which is the highest plane of transcendental wisdom and perfect understanding.

'Beyond this world, and beyond all other worlds,' he continued, 'there is an all-perfect light. It is pure intelligence, ecstasy, peace and happiness! It is the light that shines beyond darkness, time, space and dimensionality. In that all-perfect light there is no pain, suffering or limitation of any kind.

'Enlightenment is the experience of that endless and perfect light. There isn't, however, any way that the experience of enlightenment can be conveyed in words. The closest you can come to knowing what it is like, without being enlightened yourself, of course, is to meditate with an enlightened master.

'However,' Master Fwap continued, 'while I may not be able to describe to you exactly what enlightenment is like, I can tell you that it is wonderful beyond understanding. The experience of enlightenment frees your mind from painful and limited states of awareness. It is ecstasy, peace and happiness beyond measure!'

After Master Fwap explained to me why he couldn't describe what enlightenment was like, he resumed his narrative about his search for an enlightened master of his own. He told me that after many years of fruitless travelling and searching, he had inwardly resolved that if he hadn't met his master by the time he was twenty-nine, he was going to call off his search and instead find a nice Tibetan woman to settle down with.

But, as fate would have it, on the afternoon of his twenty-ninth birthday, on his way into town to look for a date, he at long last met his master.

The narration of Master Fwap's meeting with his master was interrupted when some long-haired, blond, Swedish mountain climbers picked us up and gave us a ride back to Katmandu in an old army truck. Along the way they talked with Master Fwap about how much they wanted to visit Tibet, where the borders were then closed to tourists by the Chinese Communists. Master Fwap rode in silence, listening to what they had to say, or meditating (it was hard to tell which), until we pulled up in front of the hostel.

Before we parted that day, Master Fwap gave me directions to the temple where he lived. He suggested that I visit him the next day around noon. I didn't know what to say to him. I had come to Nepal to surf the Himalayas, not to spend my time talking about enlightenment with a Buddhist monk. I thanked him very much for his invitation and also for telling me a little bit about his life, and I apologized again for having snowboarded him. But in the back of my mind I knew I wouldn't take him up on his offer to visit him the next day.

I hopped out of the truck and thanked the Swedish

driver and his friends for giving me a ride back into town. They said they were going to drive Master Fwap back to his temple. They laughingly told me it would be very bad karma not to.

CHAPTER FOUR

A Second Unusual Dream

ॐ

Undoubtedly I would not be telling you this story about my adventures as a young adult in Nepal, if I had not had a second, most unusual dream that night after returning to the hostel. After leaving Master Fwap and the Swedish mountain climbers, I entered the hostel and went in search of something to eat. I was famished from my snowboarding adventure and from my encounter and conversation with Master Fwap.

After soup, bread, and talk about politics with two French university students who had just arrived from India, I crawled into my sleeping bag and immediately fell into what was at first a deep and dreamless sleep.

Dreamless at first, but then I dreamt a dream that would change my life forever!

In my dream I was wandering lost in a snowstorm. I was alone. I felt that I was in the mountains, but I really couldn't be sure, because the snowstorm I found myself in was so severe I could barely see a few feet ahead of myself.

After walking blindly through the snow for what seemed like forever, I came upon a Buddhist temple. The door was slightly ajar. A soft yellow light came from somewhere within the temple and spilled out through the partially opened door onto the snow-covered ground that lay before me.

I walked up to the door, opened it the rest of the way and walked into the temple. Once inside, I found myself standing in a very large hall with stained glass windows and a vaulted ceiling. Looking around, I saw that the hall was lit by hundreds of small, flickering candles arranged in neat rows on iron racks attached to the walls.

Directly before me, at the front of the room, stood a large white marble altar. Six giant red candles were arranged symmetrically upon its surface. A large, colorful tapestry that had a picture of the Buddha sitting in a meditative posture on it, was hanging on the wall above the altar.

At the far end of the room, facing the altar, I saw a man sitting in a cross-legged position on the floor. His eyes were closed and he appeared to be absorbed in deep meditation. I found myself walking over to him. As I approached, he turned his head, opened his eyes and looked up at me.

Upon seeing his face, I immediately sensed that I knew him, although I couldn't quite place where or when I had met him. He beckoned to me silently, with a motion of his left hand, to come over and sit down next to him, and I did so.

We stared at each other for a long time without speaking. I saw that he was an American. He appeared to be in his late forties. He was dressed in a black business suit and had on a brightly colored tie.

'Listen to me,' he said in a deep and commanding tone.

'Tomorrow you will go to the temple and visit Master Fwap. Forget about snowboarding for now – you have something much more important to do!'

I didn't reply. I just kept staring at him, trying to figure out where I had met him before.

'You can't possibly remember where you met me before,' he said, as if he were reading my thoughts. 'So stop trying. This is the first time you have ever run into me. Don't you know who I am?'

I shook my head.

'Well, I would think it should be obvious to you,' he said with a strong laugh. 'I'm you. Not yet, of course, but in the future. The reason I'm speaking to you in this dream tonight is because you are about to make the biggest mistake in your thus-far uneventful life.'

'What's that?' I asked.

'Going snowboarding tomorrow instead of seeing Master Fwap at his temple. You owe him your life, you know. You ran him down with your snowboard on that mountain today. He could have easily burned you into a very small pile of ashes with his occult power, but because he is a compassionate Buddhist master he let you off the hook. He is a very patient man, and he is also destined to be your – our – master, and to place us on our destined path.'

'How are we doing?' I asked.

'Oh, in the future? Well, it's certainly going to be very different from what you had imagined. This place is my – our – temple. Not bad, is it? We designed it ourselves.

'Don't worry! Our future will reveal itself to you one day at a time, and that's fast enough. The point I want to make to you tonight is that you must not make a mistake by going snowboarding tomorrow. Go and see

31

Master Fwap instead. Oh, and by the way, he knows a lot more about snowboarding than you ever will!'

The room turned gold, faded and dissolved, and I awoke to my second morning in Nepal.

CHAPTER FIVE

I Visit Master Fwap

ॐ

I spent most of the early morning that day meandering through some of the shops in Katmandu. The majority of them sold inexpensive religious trinkets to tourists. But even though I was distracted by the sights and sounds of Katmandu, I couldn't quite get the dream I had of my future self out of my mind. Rather than go snowboarding that day, I decided to heed my future self's advice to seek out Master Fwap instead.

Master Fwap's temple didn't prove to be too hard to find. It was about a half-hour walk outside of central Katmandu. The directions he had given me the day before were excellent, and before I knew it, I was knocking on his temple door.

Master Fwap greeted me at the door with a big smile on his face and ushered me into the meditation hall. From there we walked to the rear of the temple to an area where his living quarters were located. He seemed very happy to see me again. He laughed and made funny sounds and remarks as we walked through the temple together.

His mood was infectious, and by the time we had reached the door to his room I was very happy to be with him again.

He opened the door to his room and led me inside. Looking around, I saw that Master Fwap's room was lit by candles, although a little bit of light also filtered in through several small windows that were up near the top of the ceiling.

His room was small and clean. It contained a bed, a writing desk with a small chair, and a meditation table that had several white candles and a small bronze figure of the Buddha on it. On the floor in front of the meditation table was a large yak-hair carpet, on which Master Fwap invited me to sit.

Master Fwap sat down on the carpet across from me. He crossed his legs in a lotus position and then neatly arranged his robes over them. He laughingly told me that he had known I would come. I decided not to bring up the dream that had brought me there. He never mentioned it, and to this day I am still unaware if he knew that I had only come to visit him because of it.

After exchanging pleasantries with me, Master Fwap picked up his narration from the previous day, continuing his story as if no time had passed since we had walked down the snowy road to Katmandu together.

Master Fwap resumed his story, telling me that he had finally encountered his long-sought-after master on the outskirts of a small town in western Tibet. Master Fwap said that as he was walking toward the town on that fateful day, in search of a date, he observed an older

Buddhist monk standing by the side of the road several meters ahead.

Just when he was about to walk past, the unknown elderly monk stepped right out in front of Master Fwap and blocked his passage into the town!

Master Fwap said that he came to an immediate stop, and out of Buddhist courtesy, he waited for the older monk to walk by him. But the unknown monk continued to stand his ground and stared fiercely, directly into Master Fwap's eyes!

It was precisely at that moment, while staring into the unknown monk's eyes, that Master Fwap had both literally and figuratively seen the light. Master Fwap whispered to me that as he stared at the unknown monk he suddenly saw thousands of waves of golden light surrounding the monk's entire body! Seeing the waves of golden auric light emanating from the aged Buddhist monk, Master Fwap intuitively realized that the unknown monk, who was blocking his passageway into town was none other than his past-life master from his previous incarnations.

Instead of going into town and finding a date as he had planned, Master Fwap and his rediscovered past-life master went off together to meditate in a nearby cave, and to catch up on old times.

Master Fwap's master, whose name was Fwaz Shastra-Dup, revealed to him that day the secret mystical teachings and techniques of the Rae Chorze-Fwaz. Information, Master Fwap told me, he in turn was going to reveal to me.

Master Fwap said that because of my karma from previous lifetimes he was going to initiate me into the innermost secret Tantric teachings of the Rae Chorze-Fwaz Buddhist Order, just as he had been initiated and been taught those same secrets and techniques by his own master, Fwaz Shastra-Dup, in a Himalayan cave on that fateful day of their multilife reunion! It was all karma, he said.

CHAPTER SIX

Master Fwap Explains Karma

ॐ

At that point I was somewhat dazed and confused by Master Fwap's sudden revelation that because of my past-life karma, he was going to initiate me into the secret Tantric Buddhist teachings of the Rae Chorze-Fwaz. I stalled Master Fwap while trying to decide whether or not I wanted to get involved with his Tantric Buddhist revelations.

To buy myself a little time, I asked Master Fwap if he would explain what karma was. I told him that, while I had heard the word used as slang hundreds of times before in California, I really had no idea what the word 'karma' meant to a Tantric Buddhist master.

Until my conversation with Master Fwap that day, it had been my understanding that 'karma' meant what you have coming to you, because of what you have done in your past. I asked Master Fwap if he would elaborate on the meaning of the word, because I was sure that my understanding of karma was probably both superficial and incorrect.

Master Fwap smiled at me for a moment and didn't say anything. I assumed he was collecting his thoughts

41

on the subject before speaking. Then, in a deep and dramatic tone, he informed me that I already knew the answer to my own question. He said all I had to do was to recollect it!

Master Fwap went on to explain that I had known all about karma, and many other mystical things, in my past lives. He said that all the knowledge from my previous incarnations was contained in what he referred to as my 'other memory.'

Master Fwap told me that if I would simply stop all my thoughts for just a few minutes and clear my mind of distracting influences, my other memory would start functioning and I would be able to answer my own question about karma.

I quickly replied that I didn't think I could stop my thoughts for even a few seconds at a time – let alone for a few minutes – and that I would very much appreciate it if he would serve as my 'other memory' for the time being. He laughed and said he would do it for me this time, but eventually I would have to learn to retrieve things from my other memory on my own.

Master Fwap Explains Karma to Me

'Karma is the way that Buddhists explain the universe,' Master Fwap began. 'Buddhists understand that today, and all other days, have turned out the way they have, because of karma.

'The past leads to the present moment, and the present moment leads to the future. The interconnection of one moment with another moment, and of one action with another action, is karma.

'Karma is what happens to you today,' Master Fwap continued. 'It is simply the law of cause and effect in action. What occurs to you today is an outgrowth of what happened yesterday. All moments and occurrences are caused by other moments and occurrences that preceded them, in an endless causal chain of karmic interactions that lead back indefinitely through time.'

'But Master Fwap!' I interjected. 'There had to be a beginning to karma at some point! Wasn't there a first moment somewhere in karmic time?'

'No,' he smiled. 'Karma has always existed, as have you, I, and all things in this wonderful universe.'

'Master Fwap, this is deep. Let me see if I correctly understand what you are saying: I exist today the way I do, and the world exists today the way it does, because of yesterday's karma; and yesterday existed the way it did, because of the day-before-yesterday's karma; and the day-before-yesterday existed the way it did, because of the preceding day's karma; and every day that has ever existed has existed the way it has, because of an endless infinity of previous karmas. Is that more or less correct, Master Fwap?'

'Exactly!' he said, nodding his neatly shaved bald head in affirmation.

'So does that mean that everything is fated, Master Fwap? If what occurs in this moment sets up the next moment, and so on forever, then there is really no such thing as free will, is there?' I asked.

'A complicated question from one who is so young,' he replied. 'I will do my best to answer it for you. You see, karma is fate, it is true! If you throw a rock up into the air, it will come down and land someplace. You might say that the place that the rock lands is its karma. But then again, it was your free choice whether or not to throw the rock up into the air in the first place.

'Everything that exists in this or any other world or dimension,' he continued, 'does so because of the way that things were in the previous moment. I call this the karma of the moment.

'But with free will, we can modify, to a certain extent, the chain of karma that has been set in motion by the karma of the previous moment. That is what free will really is. It is the ability to alter the sequence of karmic fate that was about to become our future!'

'So, Master Fwap,' I responded, 'if I understand you correctly you believe that we are the way we are because of how we were a moment ago. That moment leads to this moment, as this moment will lead to the next moment. I can understand that.

'But Master Fwap, if that's true, then how can free will exist? Isn't the choice to alter your future karma by exercising your free will now predestined by what you were thinking and feeling and by what was happening to you in the previous moment?'

Master Fwap shook his head and laughed. 'All of this is perhaps a little bit more complicated than it initially appears to be,' he replied. 'Let me try to describe the interaction of karma and free will to you in another way. Let us consider, as a way of trying to understand how karma works, who we are and how we got to be who we are.'

'You see, my young friend,' Master Fwap continued, 'karma not only means that what happens to you in the present moment is a direct outgrowth of what occurred to you in the previous moment. It also means that you are who you are right now because of who you were in the previous moment.

'Buddhists believe that you are who you are today

44

because of who you have been in all of your past lives.

'It is the Tantric Buddhist belief that today you are the product of all the moments you have lived in your current life thus far and also of all the moments, realizations and experiences you have had in all your past lives as well.

'The person you are today, the feelings you have, the thoughts you think and the way you see yourself, are all part of your past-life and present-life karmas.'

I must have had a puzzled look on my face because he paused and laughed. 'Let me use myself as an example,' he continued. 'I have always been interested in Buddhism, astrology, psychic perception, and enlightenment. I was born this way. My brothers and sisters, who grew up in the same family I did and who were exposed to the same physical and spiritual environments I was, have little or no interest in these inner matters. They are all primarily concerned with physical things that relate to their material success, such as making a living and raising a family.

'My brothers and sisters and I all had the same biological parents. We were all raised in the same way. But each of us is very different. That is our karma – who we were born as, and also who we grew up to be.

'Death is not the end of who we are,' Master Fwap said in a warm and intimate tone. 'It is only a brief pause in the endless cycle of our lives.

'Each of us is a spirit that cannot die. Our spirit grows and develops traits in each incarnation that it passes through, and then collects and carries the essence of those traits into future lifetimes. In Buddhist Yoga we refer to our multilife karmic traits as 'samskaras.' They are the internal karmic patterns that make each of us who and what we are.

45

'When we are born into a new lifetime,' he continued, 'our spirit doesn't lose the samskaras that were developed in previous incarnations. At first they are usually hidden by the temporary amnesia of infancy and by the transient personality that is assumed during childhood and adolescence. But as we grow older and mature in each incarnation, we are drawn back by samskaras – multilife karmic patterns – to previous interests and pursuits. This causes each of us to become the same kind of person we were in our past lives.

'We are born into this lifetime, as the person that we were at the moment of our death in our last lifetime. Our adult personality is a mirror image of who we were in the last stage of our life in our previous incarnation.'

I could tell by the smile on Master Fwap's face that he knew I had absolutely no idea what he was talking about. After a brief period of silence, Master Fwap tried yet another approach to enlighten me on the subject of karma.

'Try thinking of it this way,' Master Fwap began. 'Children go to school in the winter. In the summer they stay at home. When they return to school the next fall they resume their education in a higher grade because of the school work and the grade they completed the previous year.

'While it is true that a child may have developed some new ideas or interests during the course of the previous school year, or over the summer, or even may have changed their views on several subjects, the essence of the child's personality will have remained the same. Although the child is now in a new and higher grade, and may now know new things and have had many new and different experiences, the child is still the same child.

'In much the same way, whatever you have learned in your previous incarnations is retained within your "causal body" – your multi-lifetime body of energy that lives from one incarnation to another.

'It is your causal body that is the real you! At the end of each incarnation, it carries the knowledge and karmic patterns of that particular lifetime, in addition to the knowledge and karmic patterns of all of your other previous lifetimes, into your next incarnation.

'Death is only a summer vacation for us!' Master Fwap exclaimed. 'We don't really change or lose what we have learned or who we have been when we die, because we are our karma.

'The choices we make and the thoughts we allow ourselves to think, the emotions that we let run through our bodies and minds and the interests we pursue, these are the things that shape and define the spirit. That is what karma is really made of.'

Master Fwap paused for a moment to examine me. He arched his eyebrows slightly and then looked directly into my eyes. He must have been at least partially satisfied by what he saw there, because he smiled, bowed his head, and then said jokingly, 'Buddha's name be praised!' Then, after several minutes of silence, he resumed his discussion of karma with me.

'So, for example, in my case, in my last several dozen lifetimes I was a teacher of Buddhist enlightenment. I was enlightened, and I helped others who were interested in self-discovery to advance along the pathway to enlightenment in each of my enlightened lifetimes.

'The reason I was enlightened in my last several dozen incarnations was that many, many thousands of incarnations ago, of my own free will, I became interested in self-discovery and in the study of enlightenment. I studied meditation and learned all about the inner worlds and the higher dimensions from great Buddhist masters who knew about these matters.

'One lifetime led to another. In each lifetime, after first passing through the amnesia of infancy and childhood, the inclinations and memories from my past lives would resurface. Once this happened. I was irresistibly drawn back to the study of meditation and enlightenment. In one particular incarnation, I became enlightened, and I have regained and refined my enlightenment in every incarnation I have had since that time!

'However, in my current lifetime, on the fateful day of my twenty-ninth birthday, when I had just met my past-life master, Fwaz Shastra-Dup, outside of that little town in Tibet, I had absolutely no idea I had ever been enlightened in any of my previous incarnations.

'Naturally, Master Fwaz Shastra-Dup, who was a fully enlightened Buddhist master, saw and understood my past-life karma better than I did at the time. He explained all about karma to me in a cave that day, just as I am explaining karma to you here in this temple today.

'Master Fwaz Shastra-Dup told me that I had been enlightened in my past lives,' Master Fwap continued. 'He then taught me how to use the secret and powerful meditation techniques of the Rae Chorze-Fwaz. After practicing the techniques each day for many years, coupled with my master's spiritual guidance and auric empowerments, I was able to bring my past-life enlightenment back. Later, because it was also my karma, Master Fwaz made me his successor.

'This all happened to me in this lifetime because of the things I had learned and the choices I had made in my previous incarnations. What I have learned and done in my past lives and in this lifetime, is what I have become. This is the secret of what karma really is!'

'But Master Fwap, I still don't understand the difference between karmic fate and free will. Wasn't it your karma to meet your past-life master, and to regain your enlightenment, because of the fact that you had been enlightened in your previous lifetimes?'

'Yes, that is true,' he replied. 'But it was through the exercise of my free will in the first place that I began the study of meditation. That, and other choices I made to follow and stay on the pathway to enlightenment, led to my first enlightened incarnation, and also to my subsequent enlightened incarnations.

'You see,' he continued, 'free will exists and operates outside of causality. It is not hooked to karma.

'Free will is like a well that is on your property. You can choose to draw water from the well or not. That is up to you. The well will still be there whether or not you choose to use it.

'Free will exists within each of us,' Master Fwap stated factually. 'Most people choose not to use their free will, so consequently they rarely alter their karmic patterns.

'For most individuals, each new lifetime is a mirror image of the individual's previous incarnation,' Master Fwap explained. 'But if you choose to draw from the inner well of free will, then you can make choices that are outside your current karmic patterns.

'You can alter the structure of your samskaras, and of your current and future incarnations,' Master Fwap said emphatically. 'By choosing to use your free will today, you can become someone vastly different from the person you have been thus far in this life, or the persons you have been in any other lifetimes that you have ever lived!

'Advanced Buddhist Yoga is the art of altering your karmic patterns,' Master Fwap continued. 'Through the practice of meditation, and with the auric empowerments and guidance of an enlightened master, you can totally change your karmic destiny.

'By practicing Buddhist Yoga, you can become happy,

ecstatic and free in your current incarnation, even if you have never been that way before in any of your past lives, or thus far in your current life. Believe me, this is true! If there wasn't a way around the samskaras, no one would ever become enlightened!

'Remember,' Master Fwap said, lifting his hands in front of his chest to emphasize what he was saying, 'karma exists within causality. It is three-dimensional. Free will exists outside of causality; it is not bound by karma.

'By exercising your free will, thinking happier thoughts, making happier choices, and by learning and following the Buddhist way, you can totally change your karma forever. You can reshape your spirit and become a new and more ecstatic being.'

I asked Master Fwap why we all weren't born knowing about our past lives. I reasoned out loud that if we all had lived before we should simply remember our past lives from the moment that we were born, in the same way that we remember something today that we experienced yesterday.

He responded that most human beings who have been spiritually evolved in their past lives go through a stage he called 'unknowing,' during which they experience a temporary state of 'spiritual amnesia'. He told me that 'unknowing' normally lasts from birth through adolescence.

During this phase, he explained, even a very spiritually advanced person would often act just like an average child or adolescent.

'One day,' Master Fwap said, 'a person who has attained advanced levels of mind in past lives begins to remember . . . and spiritual knowledge and talents from past lives begin to resurface into the person's current self.

50

'As the memories and awareness from past lives flood into a person's current life,' he continued, 'that person goes through profound metamorphoses, and gains a totally different personality.

'During this metamorphosis, people usually lose interest in superficial things like possessions and relationships, and instead suddenly find themselves drawn to the study of the ancient, eternal and metaphysical truths. As they enter more deeply into this phase, they become calm, happy and centered, focused on the transcendental rather than the transitory.

'When a person who has had highly evolved past lives is going through a strong past-life transit, and is pulling up other-life memory from those prior lifetimes, that person comes to know things about life, death and other dimensions that most people in our world aren't aware of. Very often while this is happening, the person also rapidly regains and begins to employ past-life psychic powers, and to do things with them that defy description.'

After another period of silence, Master Fwap told me that most people who had been enlightened in their previous incarnations would normally begin to regain their past-life enlightenment – if they lived at sea level – at around the age of twenty-nine, when their astrological Saturn return took place. He said that living in or near sacred mountains, because of their beneficial auric influences, often made past-life returns happen even faster.

ॐ

CHAPTER SEVEN

I Ask a Question

I asked Master Fwap how he could be so sure that all of this was true. How did he know that it all wasn't just fantasy?

He told me that he could 'see' everything he had told me was true because his third eye was open. He said someday, after practicing meditation for many years, my third eye would also open, and then I would be able to 'see' anything in the universe I wanted to, just as he could.

CHAPTER EIGHT

The Secret of the
Rae Chorze-Fwaz

ॐ

That afternoon, while I was seated on the yak-hair rug
in his small but comfortable room, Master Fwap told me
the 'secret' of the Rae Chorze-Fwaz. It wasn't exactly a
'secret,' like something you keep hidden from others;
instead, it was more like the secret of how something
works, for instance, the 'secret' of how a jet plane flies.

Master Fwap told me that the 'secret' of the Rae
Chorze-Fwaz concerned their special meditation techniques for attaining enlightenment extremely rapidly.
He said the Rae Chorze-Fwaz had preserved and passed
on their secret meditation techniques, in oral tradition,
from the time of Atlantis until the present day.

And that is where the real story of the Rae Chorze-Fwaz,
Master Fwap, Master Fwap's master (Fwaz Shastra-
Dup), myself and you, the reader of my Himalayan
adventures that occurred when I was a young man,
begins to get just a little bit cosmically complicated.

ॐ

According to Master Fwap, the Rae Chorze-Fwaz was a Mystery School, a school where the mysteries of the universe were taught. Master Fwap patiently explained to me that a Mystery School is an occult order comprised of people who study meditation, enlightenment and psychic and occult arts.

Master Fwap told me that the Rae Chorze-Fwaz had been in existence for millennia. He explained that the members of the Order traced their origins back through Tibet, Japan, China, India and ancient Egypt to the place where the Order was founded – the lost continent of Atlantis.

Master Fwap recounted that long before the advent of what the scientists and scholars of our day consider to be the beginning of human civilization, there was an age undreamed of: the Age of Atlantis.

Atlantis, according to Master Fwap, was a highly evolved civilization where the sciences and arts were far more advanced than one might guess. He told me that, in addition to being technically advanced in genetic engineering, computer science and interdimensional physics and artistically developed in electronic music and crystal art forms, almost all of the people who lived in Atlantis meditated and had powerful psychic skills.

Master Fwap further explained that a group of highly evolved Atlantean men and women – the high priests and priestesses of Atlantis – had discovered, through their meditation practices, many of the deepest secrets of the universe. Through meditation and astral travel they had come to understand all about reincarnation, karma, and the innermost workings of the Enlightenment Cycle.

In a hushed voice, Master Fwap recounted how, in their meditations, the high priests and priestesses of Atlantis had seen that the Atlantean civilization was going to end cataclysmically. He said that, knowing the imminent destruction of Atlantis was rapidly approaching, the high priests and priestesses wanted to preserve and protect the mystical knowledge they had gained from their meditation practices and pass it on to future civilizations they clairvoyantly saw were going to be born after the destruction of Atlantis.

Because the high priests and priestesses of Atlantis could 'see' through their third eyes, Master Fwap explained, they knew exactly when and how their continent was going to be destroyed.

The night before Atlantis sank beneath the waves forever, the members of the Mystery School set sail from their doomed continent in twelve boats, headed for twelve different points on the globe. Master Fwap told me it was their intention to start twelve new civilizations similar to Atlantis in these locations.

'Unfortunately,' Master Fwap said nostalgically, 'half the boats – along with their passengers and crews – were lost in a great storm at sea, and many members of the six boats that did make it to their destinations safely, were later killed by the very native peoples to whom they sought to transmit their knowledge of the Atlantean sciences, arts and metaphysics.

'The only group of Atlanteans that was truly successful in transplanting their knowledge to a new location,' Master Fwap added, 'was the group that landed in what is now Egypt.

'Once the members of the Rae Chorze-Fwaz had established themselves in Egypt,' he continued, 'they found and educated people there to whom they eventually transmitted their secret techniques and knowledge.'

At that point, I interrupted Master Fwap's chronicle of his mystical Order, and inquired why all of this was necessary to begin with. I reasoned that even if all of the members of the Rae Chorze-Fwaz in Atlantis had died when their continent had sunk, or had been lost in small boats at sea afterwards, they would have soon reincarnated and remembered everything anyway.

Master Fwap said that unfortunately past-life remembrance wasn't quite that simple, and in order for me to properly understand why this was so, I needed a brief course in the earth's energy cycles and auric patterning.

CHAPTER NINE

Master Fwap's Brief Course in the Earth's Cycles and Auric Patterning

'Everyone is psychic!' Master Fwap declared with a broad smile. 'When your mind is clear and focused, and if there aren't too many people in your immediate vicinity, you can feel all kinds of wonderful things! You can feel the brightness of eternity and the ecstasy of creation. You can see the light of enlightenment inside of everything!

'When your mind is clear and your third eye is open, you can see and know things that are taking place thousands of miles away from you. You can know what other people are thinking about you, or what is coming at you – and decide whether or not you want to experience it!

'During the time of Atlantis, members of the Mystery School discovered and developed specific concentration exercises that they found would radically increase and sharpen their innate psychic abilities. These techniques, when properly employed, allowed them to control and suspend their thought processes for prolonged periods of time.'

Master Fwap then explained to me that by suspending thought for protracted periods – a practice that he and other modern day Buddhist masters refer to as meditation – an individual can perceive and have direct experiences in countless non-physical worlds and dimensions.

'The members of the Atlantean Mystery School were the earliest human explorers of the frontiers of inner space!' Master Fwap exclaimed jubilantly. 'Through their internal meditative journeys and explorations, they discovered many secret astral passageways that led to an infinite variety of other worlds and dimensions.'

'Are those worlds and dimensions as solid and real as our world, Master Fwap?' I asked.

'Why yes, of course they are,' he replied. 'As a matter of fact, some of those dimensions are much more "real" than this universe is!'

I interrupted him again: 'But how can that be, Master Fwap? Nothing can be more real than the physical world. Isn't that what the word "real" means to begin with?'

'Reality is perhaps a more complicated concept than you might imagine,' he quickly replied. 'In our Far Eastern languages we have many different words to describe the varying degrees of reality that a thing, a state of mind or a plane of being may have.'

'But I still don't see, Master Fwap, how one object or world can be more real than another!' I protested.

'You are having trouble understanding this concept because you are thinking in English!' Master Fwap said. 'The language you think in can limit your ability to understand something like this.'

'What do you mean by that, Master Fwap? Now you are really confusing the issue by blaming it on semantics!' I was beginning to get frustrated by my lack of understanding, and for some unknown reason I felt that Master Fwap was intentionally making his explanation more complicated and abstruse than was really necessary.

'Consider the word "love" as an example,' Master Fwap calmly responded. 'Now, as you know, love is an emotion. In your English language you have just a single word for what is perhaps one of the most complex feelings in all of eternity.

'But there are thousands of types of love, aren't there?' he continued. 'There is romantic love, family love, friendship, flirtation, parental love, the love of God and the spirit, jealous and possessive love, selfless love, innocent love, multiple-life love and so on. As a matter of fact, no two people ever experience love in exactly the same way.

'But in English you have just one word for something that is so complicated. In other languages, however, there are sometimes dozens or even hundreds of different words for the degrees and types of love that human beings can experience.'

'But what does that have to do with different degrees of reality?' I complained.

'Everything and nothing,' Master Fwap responded at once. 'Don't allow yourself to get frustrated so easily. Give me a few more moments of your time, and I think you will understand what I mean.

'You see, my young friend, language is the medium of our thoughts. Thoughts can increase our understanding of a subject, or they can just as easily constrict or block our understanding of a subject. It very much depends upon the language that we are thinking in.

'If the language that we think in doesn't have the right words for what we are trying to understand or express, it's like trying to put a square peg into a round hole!

'So,' he continued, 'if you have only one word for all the colors of love, then you may begin to "think" love instead of feeling it. You may take it for granted that when you think the word "love," you already know and have experienced all of its possible permutations.'

'Let me see if I understand you correctly, Master Fwap. In other words, when I think the word "love" in my mind, you are suggesting I have a concept for love that is based upon my past experiences and associations with love, and that this concept will stop me from experiencing other types of love, unless I have additional words at my disposal that define different gradations of love. Is that what you mean?'

'Exactly!' he replied with a broad smile.

'But if that is the case, Master Fwap,' I continued, in a mock argumentative fashion, 'why would thinking the word "love" in any way curtail new and different feelings of love, as they would spontaneously arise within me? Wouldn't the new types of love I feel and experience for people, places and things modify and expand the meaning of the word "love" for me?'

At this point, I was getting a little bit giddy. Everything that had seemed so frustrating to me just moments before, had somehow suddenly taken on a comic tone. It seemed to me that Master Fwap and I were both taking part in a ludicrous mock debate, of absurd proportions, similar to the one that had taken place at the Mad Hatter's tea party, in *Alice in Wonderland*.

'Master Fwap, does thinking a word stop me from experiencing what the word describes?' I asked.

'Yes and no,' he replied.

'Which part is yes and which part is no?'

'Do you know much about Zen Buddhism?' Master

Fwap inquired, with what I perceived to be a deceptively wry smile.

'No, not really. Tell me about it.'

'It is the method of knowing the mind through its own emptiness.'

'What does that mean, Master Fwap?'

'Zen Buddhists believe that when we think about something conceptually, we cut ourselves off from its true essence. From a Zen point of view, it is only by going beyond our limited concept of something, and experiencing its "suchness," or essential nature, that we really come to know what a thing, experience or understanding truly is.

'The Zen Buddhist monks use concentration techniques to rid themselves of concepts. They believe enlightenment lies just beyond words, in the things and experiences of daily life that are right in front of us at every moment. In short, according to Zen doctrine, happiness comes when we rid ourselves of the concepts that society, language and structured thinking have given us.

'There is an old Zen saying,' Master Fwap continued. 'Before enlightenment, chop wood and carry water; after enlightenment, chop wood and carry water.'

Master Fwap paused and waited for me to respond.

'What does that mean?' I hesitantly inquired.

'It means that enlightenment doesn't really change anything, yet it changes everything; or you might say that enlightenment changes everything without changing anything.'

'Master Fwap, are you deliberately trying to confuse me?'

'No,' he replied with a good-natured laugh, 'I am not deliberately trying to confuse you at all. Actually I don't think that I have to. You've been doing a pretty good job of confusing yourself all of your life.'

'What does that phrase mean then? I don't understand it!'

'It's a way of trying to explain what enlightenment is and isn't.' Master Fwap responded. 'Most people who read about or study enlightenment have a preconceived notion of what enlightenment is. Naturally that concept, like all concepts, is limited by the words that make it up. So this phrase explains that enlightenment is not a concept.

'Before enlightenment,' Master Fwap continued, 'the Zen Buddhist monk chopped wood and carried water. After he became enlightened, he continued to chop wood and carry water.

'Most people assume,' Master Fwap continued, 'that after they become enlightened, their outer lives will magically change. They imagine that they will suddenly dress in flowing robes, give up working, and spend their time sitting on top of a mountain meditating in bliss all day.'

'Well, wouldn't you, Master Fwap? I mean, what good would enlightenment be if it didn't change your life? Isn't that why people seek enlightenment, to get away from the boredom and frustration of their daily experiences?'

'Exactly!' Master Fwap replied. 'That's what most people think! But that is not necessarily the case. You see, enlightenment allows you to perceive things differently. Perception is the key to everything!

'Before the Zen monk became enlightened, chopping wood and carrying water seemed like mundane, repetitious and boring tasks to him. But after he became enlightened, his perception of chopping wood and carrying water, and of everything else in life, radically changed. He discovered that enlightenment exists in chopping wood and carrying water, as much as it also does in sitting on top of a mountain top and meditating all day.

'Before you become enlightened,' Master Fwap continued patiently, 'the world appears to be three-dimensional, dull and boring. But in reality, the world is not three-dimensional, and if you are at all aware, it is anything but boring.

'Life is composed of millions of dimensions. To an awakened mind, life and even the most repetitive tasks in daily living, can never be dull and boring at all, because infinity exists in all things!

'Before he became enlightened, the monk's thoughts, concepts and mental routines blocked his perception of the infinite brightness that exists within all things.

'After his enlightenment, while the monk's body might still have been chopping wood and carrying water, his mind was constantly roaming through the ecstatic dimensions of light. So the point of the Zen phrase is that enlightenment is not what you think it is, because enlightenment is beyond the power of your thoughts and ability to understand.

'Once you have become enlightened,' Master Fwap said dramatically, 'you don't have to live in a monastery, because the whole universe has become your monastery. You can lead a normal life doing whatever you choose.

'Physically it might appear that nothing remarkable has changed in your day-to-day life. But within your mind, you will live in a condition of continuous light and ecstasy, just like the Zen monk.'

'But Master Fwap, I still don't understand how some types of reality can be more real than others!'

'Once you get beyond your conception of what reality is,' Master Fwap said, 'you will transcend the words and concepts you have already developed for reality.

It's really that easy. But as long as you continue to "think" life, instead of directly experiencing it in a nonconceptual way, you will not understand any more about reality than you do today.

'So,' he remarked, 'let us forget for a few minutes that we have a preconceived understanding of what the word "real" means. Let's start from scratch, and through observation determine what is real and what is not. Let's find out, by directly examining life, if some things have more reality than other things.'

At that point in our discussion Master Fwap paused. 'How would you define reality? What, in your opinion, makes something real?'

'Well, I suppose something is real because it exists,' I replied.

'But things don't exist, or if they do exist, they only exist for a fleeting moment.'

'What do you mean by that, Master Fwap?'

'Well, the only thing that exists is this moment, right here and now!' Master Fwap said emphatically. 'There is no past,' he continued, 'not past any given moment that is still taking place. The past, whether it was thousands of years ago or just a few seconds ago, only exists as an idea or impression in our memory.'

'So then, what is real isn't real for more than a fleeting moment. Is that what you are saying?' I inquired.

'Exactly so!' he swiftly replied. 'And to complicate matters even further, the reality of a thing depends entirely upon your perception of it, and your perception of an event only lasts for an instant before it fades into memory.'

'Master Fwap, I think this is getting a little too metaphysical for me. I'm starting to get a headache!' I said in a sudden outburst.

'Try thinking of it this way,' he continued, ignoring my

overly emotional statement. 'What makes something real to begin with is the fact that it exists. We both agree that when something doesn't exist, it isn't real. So suppose some things exist longer than other things do. Would you say that makes them more real?'

'I suppose so,' I reluctantly agreed.

'Enlightened Buddhist masters know that nothing in the physical or astral worlds exists for more than a moment at a time. But they also know that nirvana exists continuously; it is a constant. So therefore nirvana – which is enlightenment – is certainly more real than anything physical or astral, because it never ends.

'The only constant outside of nirvana is change,' Master Fwap continued. 'Nothing remains the same from one moment to the next moment, in this or any other dimension. You may think that things do, but that is a trick of your thoughts and conceptions.

'All things and beings are made up of vibrating energy,' he continued. 'Nothing in the universe is really as solid as it looks. For example, an unenlightened person sees a tree as something solid and tangible. But an enlightened person looks at a tree, and sees an ever-changing continuum of energy, that is currently taking the form of a tree.

'The universe is made up of endless dimensional planes,' Master Fwap said strongly. 'Some planes are more durable than others, and of course nirvana is beyond change. So the closer a plane of being is to nirvana, in a way of speaking, the more real it is. Conversely, the farther away from nirvana something is, the less real it is.'

'But Master Fwap, I thought you said that nirvana wasn't spatial. It's not really a physical place, is it? If that is the case, then how can one dimension be closer to it, or another be farther from it?'

'You are absolutely correct,' Master Fwap swiftly responded. 'Nirvana is not spatial, not in the way that you mean, anyway. I know that, as frustrating as it may be for you, there is really no way to explain nirvana at all. Words are useless.

'Nirvana is something you have to experience directly in order to know it,' Master Fwap elucidated. 'And nirvana is not something you can know directly, in the way you can know a person, know how to do something, or know and understand a concept.

'The knowing of nirvana is nonconceptual knowledge,' he continued. 'That is why, in Buddhist philosophy, we say nirvana is the wisdom beyond the mind's knowing.

'We meditate and practice mindfulness to go beyond the limited concepts that keep us in relatively unreal states of mind,' Master Fwap said with a twinkle in his eyes. 'Beyond the limited states of mind most human beings experience, there are more durable levels of perception that exist in the astral and the causal planes.

'When you experience these more "real" levels of perception you will be happy all of the time! So the members of the Atlantean Mystery School practiced meditation, and discovered there are varying degrees of reality in the universe. In addition, they also discovered that internal harmony directly affects a person's ability to perceive and experience enlightened states of consciousness.'

Master Fwap Resumes His Narrative

'In and through their internal study and metaphysical research, the members of the Mystery School discovered

70

there was a strong relationship between one's state of mind, and one's level of psychic attainment. They found that an individual who wasn't happy, emotionally in control, balanced, funny, and at peace with himself, couldn't fully develop his innate psychic powers.

'The reason for this is deceptively simple.' Master Fwap said with a laugh. 'All psychic and spiritual development is dependent upon an invisible internal energy called "prana." Prana – which is sometimes also called "kundalini" or "chi" – is the energy of consciousness. The amount of prana that people store within themselves determines both their level of day-to-day awareness, and also their ability to use their psychic and occult powers.

'Prana is stored in an internal "reservoir" inside a person's subtle body,' Master Fwap continued. 'Certain activities like meditating, visiting places of power, and being empowered by an enlightened master increase the amount of prana a person has.

'There are also ways of thinking, acting and feeling that quickly use up stored prana and unnecessarily waste it. The fastest ways to burn up and waste prana are to experience unhappiness, hate, anger, depression, self-pity and egotism.

'When people's lives are in a continual state of emotional and mental upheaval,' Master Fwap explained, 'they lose almost all of their prana, even if they meditate and engage in other internal practices that increase their psychic energy level every day.

'Without the internal energy that stored prana provides, people cannot develop their higher psychic perceptions, let alone gain siddha powers and become enlightened.

'In addition to learning how certain types of emotion and behavior could burn up or increase prana,' Master

71

Fwap continued, in a tone that a university professor might use to address a large gathering of his students, 'the members of the Atlantean Mystery School also discovered the importance of keeping themselves aurically pure and clear from the thought forms, desires, fears and negative emotions of others.

'They observed that most individuals, without consciously realizing it, absorb a great deal of psychic energy from the people they casually associate with, and an even a greater amount of psychic energy from the people with whom they have strong emotional connections.

'The energies and mental states that we psychically pick up from the people we are emotionally close to, or those with whom we physically interact, build up on our subtle body, in much the same way that dirt builds up on our physical body during the course of a day.

'If these negative auric vibrations are not kept to a minimum by using psychic shielding techniques, and if they aren't cleansed from our subtle body each day through the practice of meditation, they will accumulate and eventually become extremely toxic!

'The buildup of negative auric vibrations initially impairs our ability to perceive psychically,' he continued to elucidate. 'If these energies build up over a long period of time, they can eventually cause us to become physically ill. Most serious illnesses, including many types of cancer, are the result of auric toxicity.'

ॐ

Master Fwap went on to explain that the secret knowledge of enlightenment is like a flame. He said the first people to become enlightened in Atlantis had, in effect, lit the 'flame of enlightenment' on earth for the first time. The members of the various Mystery Schools of spiritual and psychic development had kept that flame of enlightenment alive by preserving and passing on – from generation to generation – the secret techniques for attaining enlightenment, from the time of Atlantis to our present day. He said the Rae Chorze-Fwaz was the most recent Tibetan incarnation of the Mystery Schools of the past.

Master Fwap also informed me that during the Atlantean Cycle, the earth's aura – the invisible astral energy field that surrounds and protects our planet and through which all psychic perception flows – was very pure. He compared the earth's aura to its ozone layer.

'The earth's ozone layer,' Master Fwap continued, 'is an invisible shield that protects human beings and other living things from the sun's ultraviolet radiation. If the earth's ozone layer ever becomes severely depleted, most plant and animal life on our planet will perish.

'In a similar way, all living things have an aura, a rapidly vibrating, invisible psychic energy field that protects them from toxic, non-physical energies that would otherwise be detrimental to them.

'During the age of Atlantis, there were only several hundred thousand people living on our planet. They lived in a sublime state of harmony with nature. At that time, because of the purity of the earth's aura, it was much easier to meditate, to be in touch with the spiritual side of your being, and to become enlightened.

'Think of it this way,' Master Fwap continued. 'If you want to hear music on the radio, you simply have to tune in to a station and listen to what is playing. But if hundreds and thousands of stations were all jamming the air waves at the same time, you wouldn't be able to hear any of them. Even if they were all playing the most beautiful music, you would only hear a dissonant white noise coming out of your radio.

'Every living being is psychic!' he exclaimed. 'Whether or not we are consciously aware of it, we all feel vibrations and energies coming to us from other people all of the time. We feel these things with our aura, the outermost layer of our subtle bodies.

'Did you know that the vast majority of the thoughts you think and the emotions you feel aren't even your own?' Master Fwap asked with a wry smile on his face.

'As I mentioned to you before,' he reminded me, 'you pick up most of your thoughts and emotions psychically, from the people you are physically near, and also from people for whom you have strong positive or negative emotional feelings. In addition, you also pick up psychic impressions from where you work or go to school, the roads you drive on, the stores you shop in, the city and the country you live in, and, to a certain extent, from all of the people who live on our very crowded planet.'

'In what way are we affected by other people's vibratory impressions, Master Fwap?'

'Well, let us suppose that you live next to an alcoholic. You might suddenly find yourself wanting to drink. If you follow that feeling, which was not yours to begin with, you might start to drink on a regular basis. Then, in an intoxicated haze, you might neglect your work, get mad at the people you care about, or even get into a car accident. In short, if you followed the feelings of the alcoholic next door, without realizing they weren't your own feelings, you could ruin your entire life!

'Or let us say,' Master Fwap continued, 'that you love someone who is very depressed. Even though that person may live in a different part of the country than

74

you do, you may find yourself thinking and feeling that person's unhappy thoughts and depressed emotions, even though you might be a very happy person.

'Psychic impressions can also remain in a physical location for some time. If a newly married couple who were very happy with each other moved into a home just vacated by a couple whose marriage had ended in divorce, the newlyweds might find themselves fighting with each other all of the time, even though they really loved one another!

'Without either of them consciously realizing it, the newlyweds could easily pick up the thought forms of the previous tenants of the house, assume these were their own thoughts and feelings, and act upon them.

'In addition to the vibratory effect that individuals who are physically near can have upon us,' Master Fwap explained, 'and the even stronger effect that people to whom we are emotionally close have, we are also affected by the collective consciousness of all of humanity's vibrations.

'You see, every person's mind acts like a radio transmitter: it constantly transmits the essence of their thoughts and emotions into the earth's aura. Now that the earth's population has grown well into the billions, there are so many people's thought forms psychically flooding the earth's aura that it has become highly toxic! Because of this psychic pollution of the earth's aura, it has become very difficult even for individuals with a highly developed psychic facility to perceive things clearly.

'It might be easier for you to understand what I am talking about if you were to try an experiment,' Master Fwap said.

'Observe how many thoughts you think when you are around other people. Then go for a walk in the woods, on an empty beach, in the desert or on a mountain.

'When you perform this experiment, try not to walk on a trail or beach that people tend to walk on or visit frequently. As I mentioned before, a certain amount of a person's thought forms are left in the physical locations that the person frequents. Instead, try walking on a trail or a beach that is not as well worn, or depart from the trail to a pure spot where no one has recently been, and spend a few minutes there by yourself.

'After you have spent ten or twenty minutes in a relatively pure spot,' Master Fwap continued, 'observe your mind. You will probably notice that you are neither thinking as much as you were before, nor are you thinking the same types of thoughts that you were earlier, when other people were around you. This change in the quantity and quality of your thoughts has occurred because you have physically distanced yourself from others, and also because the natural elements in the forests, mountains, deserts, and near oceans and other large bodies of water, help shield you from the thought forms and auras of other human beings.'

'Master Fwap, I still don't understand how all this relates to my question,' I said impatiently. 'Why couldn't the members of the Mystery School who died during the destruction of Atlantis, or afterwards in their boats, simply reincarnate, go into their other memories, and recall everything they had known in Atlantis?'

'You should be able to answer that question for yourself, now that I have explained how the aura works,' Master Fwap replied.

'I don't know! It's too confusing! Would you please explain it to me in a simpler way?'

Master Fwap smiled sympathetically. 'It's easy to understand. Just put all the facts that I have given you together.'

I remained silent. I didn't have any idea how to

answer my own question. After waiting patiently for my non-forthcoming response, Master Fwap sighed and proceeded to answer my question.

'During the age of Atlantis,' he said, 'the low population density – and the resulting purity of the earth's aura – made conditions ideal for discovering the secret meditation techniques for the first time. But the destruction of Atlantis happened to coincide with an overall rise in the population of other less technically and spiritually evolved civilizations on the earth.

'So by the time the Egyptian civilization had begun to flourish,' Master Fwap continued to explain, 'the earth's aura had already become so dense that it was impossible to discover the secret meditation techniques – as had been done so easily in the auric purity of the first age of Atlantis.

'This was the primary reason the Mystery School was formed. The first members of the Order, during the time of Atlantis, had psychically seen the subsequent ages of auric darkness that the earth was going to lapse into. They knew that the vibratory toxicity of these subsequent ages would make it impossible for reincarnating members of the Order to go deeply enough into their other memories, and recall what they had known in Atlantis, without knowing the secret techniques first.'

'So,' I inquired, 'they needed the secret techniques to jump-start their other memories, and someone had to be around who knew the secret techniques to teach the reincarnating members of the Order how to use them after they were reborn into a new incarnation. Is that the idea, Master Fwap?'

'Exactly. That is why there must always be at least one member of the Order on earth to orally pass the techniques on to others who have recently reincarnated. Then, by employing the secret techniques, newly incarnated members, or whomever the techniques may be taught to, can go ahead and access their other memories, and recall everything from their past lives for themselves.'

'Master Fwap, how did all of this work in Atlantis? Were children born just knowing all of this because the aura of the earth was so pure?'

'In Atlantis,' Master Fwap responded, 'children who were spiritually evolved from meditative practices in their previous lives were brought to the Mystery School for training by older members of the Order who psychically recognized them. At the Temple of Atlantis, the high priests and priestesses taught the children the secret meditation techniques, along with methods and ways of living that would increase their pranic levels and help them develop their psychic skills.

'The Mystery School continued to perform this service throughout the greater Egyptain civilization – which, as I mentioned before, was the second age of humankind – and later, on into the third age of humankind, when the Indian, Chinese, Japanese and Tibetan high cultures flourished.

'But the tremendous increase in the world's population during the third age has made meditation and psychic perception – things that should be easy and come naturally to spiritually evolved people – difficult to practice and participate in.

'All of the billions of people who now inhabit our planet are putting a terrific strain not only on the earth's natural resources, but also on its aura, making it difficult, if not impossible, even for evolved people to become aware of their past-life knowledge and talents.

'You must understand that enlightenment,' Master Fwap continued, 'is a perfect state of mind. When you are enlightened, you hear and feel ecstasy – the music of the universe – all the time! Ecstasy is always present, but we are usually so psychically blocked up by our thoughts, our negative emotions, our ego's machinations, and the auras of others, that we are completely unaware of it. Instead of feeling the innately enlightened and ecstatic nature of all things, we tend to get caught up in our thoughts, emotions and in the idiotic and idiosyncratic dramas that make up our day-to-day lives.

'To become enlightened, it is necessary to still your thoughts and emotions, and become empty,' Master Fwap said calmly. 'This is the beginning of true meditation: to empty your mind of distracting ideas, feelings and ways of looking at things – which we in the Buddhist Order refer to as illusions – and instead allow your awareness to roam through the dimensions and planes of higher light that exist deep within your mind. This is one of the goals of higher Buddhist Yoga.'

After Master Fwap had explained all this to me, he talked in more detail about the progression of the Order through Egypt, India, China, Japan, and finally into Tibet. He said that everything had gone smoothly in keeping the secret teachings and techniques alive throughout all of the untold ages of humankind until very recently.

Master Fwap told me that in 1950 the Communist Chinese had unexpectedly invaded Tibet, massacred hundreds of thousands of Tibetan Buddhist monks, and destroyed or desecrated the Tibetan monasteries. All the living members of the Rae Chorze-Fwaz, with the exception of Master Fwap – who had managed to escape to safety in Nepal – were either executed or worked to death in Chinese forced-labor camps.

So, for the first time in the history of the Order, there

was only one member left alive, Master Fwap. He alone had the full knowledge of the secret tantric techniques for rapidly attaining enlightenment.

CHAPTER TEN

Master Fwaz Shastra-Dup's Prophetic Dream

ॐ

Master Fwap told me that his own master, Fwaz Shastra-Dup, had made a significant prophecy to him about the future of the Order before the Chinese invasion of Tibet had taken place. One day, when he and Master Fwap were out hiking in the Himalayas, Fwaz Shastra-Dup told Master Fwap about a prophetic dream he had dreamt the night before.

He told Master Fwap that in his dream he had seen a time in the future when Master Fwap was going to be the only living member of the Rae Chorze-Fwaz left on the earth.

In his dream he had seen Master Fwap – the last living member of the Order – travelling in the Himalayas looking for a student to transmit the secret techniques to. He told Master Fwap that toward the end of his dream he had seen a tall, skinny young man with pale skin flying down a mountain and bumping into Master Fwap. He said that this particular young man would come from a country in the West, and that he would become Master Fwap's apprentice.

He also told Master Fwap that he had 'seen' in his dream that this new apprentice would learn the secret meditation techniques from Master Fwap, and then transmit them in a new way in a new land. As a result of this, he said, the Order was going to move its main teaching facilities from the East to the West. In addition, he told Master Fwap that from the time of the 1990s forward, the meditation techniques of the Rae Chorze-Fwaz, which up until that time had been the closely guarded secret of the members of the Order, would be transmitted to millions of young students all over the world!

Master Fwap then told me enthusiastically that he would teach me, starting the next day at noon, the secret techniques and doctrines of the Rae Chorze-Fwaz. He said that once I had learned the secret techniques, methods and philosophy of Tantric Buddhism from him, it would then be my karma to return to the West, practice the techniques for many years until I had perfected them myself, and then write a series of books that would transmit the secret techniques and teachings of the Rae Chorze-Fwaz to the students of the world.

While Master Fwap and I had been busy conversing about enlightenment and the history of the Mystery Schools, the afternoon had come and gone and it had grown cold and dark outside. Master Fwap told me that I had heard enough for one day. He advised me to return to the hostel, to eat well and get some rest, and then come back the next day at noon to his temple for further conversation about meditation and enlightenment.

As I was walking back to the hostel, a very cold wind blew against my body and it began to snow. My skin tingled as the particles of blowing snow hit my face. As I walked, I drew my parka as tightly around my body as I could.

In what seemed like no time at all, I reached the hostel and entered into its warmth and shelter. After taking off my coat, I washed, had dinner, and slept through the night without having any dreams at all.

CHAPTER ELEVEN

An Enlightening Cup of Tea

ॐ

I returned to Master Fwap's temple the next day at noon, as he had suggested. Once again Master Fwap met me at the temple door and guided me back to his quarters. We sat on the yak-hair rug in his room as we had the day before. But this time the table between us had a teapot and two empty tea cups on it.

'I have invited you for tea today,' Master Fwap began. 'I enjoy drinking tea several times a day. In fact, tea is my favorite drink. Do you like tea?'

I told him I did. He then proceeded to pour us each a steaming cup of hot tea from his teapot. I thought that it might be too hot to drink, but upon tasting it I was pleased to discover that it wasn't.

'Today I am going to teach you about enlightenment!' Master Fwap announced loudly, as if there were other people in the room whom he wanted to make aware of what he was saying. 'But before I do, I would like to answer the question that I know you are just burning to ask me.'

He paused for a moment and sipped his tea. I reflected

for a moment. If I had a particular question on my mind that I wanted to ask Master Fwap, I was certainly not conscious of it. However after a few more moments of silence, a question occurred to me.

'Master Fwap,' I began, 'I don't understand any of this. I came to Nepal to snowboard the Himalayas, not to learn about enlightenment and the secret teachings of your Buddhist Order.

'I don't mean to complain, but are you sure you have the right guy here?'

Master Fwap smiled at me and didn't say a word. Then he closed his eyes. Several minutes passed and he still didn't respond to my question. As a matter of fact, the expression on his face was so peaceful I was afraid that he might have drifted off to sleep.

As I sat on the yak-hair rug in Master Fwap's small, clean and comfortable room, a very strange thing began to occur. The air in the room began to thicken and turn a beautiful, bright golden color – not all at once, but very gradually.

At first I thought it was 'snowing' golden light around Master Fwap. I noticed the phenomenon first around his head; then the golden light seemed to spread all around his body, and finally it filled up the entire room!

Seeing the golden light surrounding Master Fwap's body, my first thought was that something must have happened to my vision. I rubbed my eyes with both of my hands in an attempt to clear my sight. But it didn't make the slightest bit of difference. The color of the air around Master Fwap and in the room remained a soft and beautiful gold.

As I watched in amazement, the golden light that was filling the room became even thicker. After a few more minutes, I could barely see Master Fwap at all, even though he was sitting directly across the table from me.

Then I felt my entire body beginning to tingle with a prickly heat. It wasn't an entirely unpleasant sensation, just unusual.

I lost consciousness of the passage of time. Master Fwap and I could have been sitting in his room for five minutes or five hours, I couldn't tell the difference. I did notice, however, that my mind had become clear, composed and relaxed. In fact I felt very good, probably better than I had ever felt before in my life.

As timeless time passed, another awareness began to overtake me: without any apparent effort on my part, I suddenly understood everything. Not that there was anything in particular to understand; I suddenly just 'knew' all about life. I realized that I was one with life, and at the same time a separate and unique part of it.

It was then that I first knew Master Fwap was enlightened. Somehow I could feel inside of his mind – and I knew it was made up of the pure golden light. I also knew, without knowing how I knew, that the golden light in Master Fwap's mind, and the golden light that was currently filling up his room, was the light of enlightenment.

I could sense that Master Fwap's mind stretched out endlessly in every direction, throughout all time, space and dimensionality. I had never felt or experienced anything that was so incredibly beautiful before.

Then Master Fwap spoke to me in a soothing tone of voice. He didn't open his eyes as he spoke.

He talked about enlightenment. As he spoke to me, the waves of golden light continued to emanate from his body in a seemingly endless variety of kaleidoscopic patterns. I noticed at times there was a steady flow of soft golden light coming directly from his body, and at other times it seemed to pulse rhythmically throughout the room, in time with his speech patterns.

'Enlightenment,' he began, 'is the complete awareness of life, without any mental modifications. It is happiness, ecstasy and all that is beautiful, perfect and fulfilling in life. Enlightenment,' he continued, 'is a perfect state of mind. It is the direct "seeing" of reality.

'The world most people see, which they call life, is really just a dream. Just as the events in a dream have an apparent solidity while you are dreaming them, so also day-to-day life seems solid and real while you are experiencing it. But when a day, an experience, or a feeling has passed, it loses its apparent solidity, just as the events in a dream lose their sense of reality after you have awakened from them.

'The world you experience every day and night of your life is transient; you – the person who experiences all of this, the people you know, have known or will one day know, the feelings and experiences you have had, are having now, or will have one day in the future, all of these things, times, places, people, experiences, understandings, feelings and events, are transient.

'They only last for the blink of an eye, and then they dissolve back into that unknowable and formless eternity from which all things come, and to which all things eventually must return.

'But behind this transient reality that comes and goes so swiftly, there is something else. It is a deeper, more permanent and unchanging reality that we Buddhists call nirvana.

'As I told you yesterday, nirvana is not really a physical place, although sometimes in conversation I talk about it as if it were. It is not really an experience, although sometimes for purposes of explanation and clarification I mention it as if it was.

'Nirvana is the intelligent light that makes us and everything that we experience, from birth to death and from death to rebirth. It is also the same light that makes up everything that is beyond the cycle of birth, death and rebirth.

'It is wonderful beyond knowing! It creates all of the transient worlds, and the beings that inhabit them, out of itself. It sustains them, transforms them, and eventually draws them back into itself again.

'And yet, while the beings it creates will experience the pleasures and pains and the successes and failures of existence, it remains aloof from them. It is untouched by their happiness or unhappiness. Nirvana is a state of perpetual bliss and ecstasy, unaffected by the transient ups and downs of its own creations!

'Tantric Buddhist Yoga is a pathway a person can follow to enlightenment. Through the tantric practices you can unite your consciousness with the eternal bliss and ecstasy of nirvana and rise above the limited conditions of pleasure and pain, success and failure, happiness and sorrow, that all of the countless unenlightened beings in creation are slaves to.

'If you want to constantly experience the unalloyed ecstasy of life, you must first break contact with the things that cause you pain. You can accomplish this through the twin Buddhist practices of meditation and mindfulness.

'In meditation, by fully focusing your mind on your chakras, stilling your thoughts, and increasing your kundalini flow, you can rise above your body consciousness and unite your mind with the clear light of nirvana. This establishes a flow of bliss and happiness between your mind and enlightenment.

'With the happiness, ecstasy and power you gain from meditation, you can then gradually remove your mind from the things it has become hooked to that cause it pain. Once you have accomplished this, regardless of what happens to you in your physical life, you will always be happy.

'When you draw your happiness each day from the endless awareness of nirvana,' Master Fwap continued, 'you are no longer a slave to fortune. When pleasant experiences come your way, you can enjoy them. But if pain and misfortune befall you, you can rise above them and remain unaffected. The bliss and ecstasy of nirvana will lift you far above the transient sorrows of both life and death.

'Try thinking of it this way,' Master Fwap said. 'Above the clouds, the sun is always shining. Today, if it is a cloudy day, we cannot enjoy the sunshine and feel as much of its warmth as we could on a sunny day. But if you and I were to get into a jet plane and fly high above the clouds, there would only be sunshine. It is always sunny above the clouds.

'In much the same way, if you derive your happiness from the events, sensations and other experiences that you have in this physical world, and from the emotions and feelings they generate within your mind and body, you are a slave to the "weather" of events. When things are "sunny" in your life you will be happy. But on "cloudy" days, which we all have in life, you will be sad, depressed and in pain.

'As you know, we cannot control the weather. As a matter of fact, we can hardly predict it. It is the same with day-to-day life. It is very hard to control life even some of the time, let alone most or all of the time, and it is almost impossible to predict life.

'But after you have united your mind with nirvana in deepest meditation, you will always be in an enlightened state of consciousness. Then let the clouds of life come! Let the rain of unhappy and tragic experiences fall, as sometimes it inevitably must, even in the lives of enlightened masters. If your mind has become one with nirvana, through the practice of meditation and mindfulness, you will remain happy at all times.'

'But Master Fwap,' I found myself asking, 'how do people who meditate feel during the period of time before they become enlightened? Are they as unhappy and do they still suffer as much as other unenlightened people, or are they better able to deal with what you refer to as the "cloudy" days of human life because they meditate? Do they have to become enlightened before things really improve for them?'

Master Fwap opened his eyes and looked directly at me. 'These are good questions!' he laughed. 'Naturally it takes quite a bit of time to become enlightened. But it is really not so different from learning any other art: all you need is time, a good teacher, and practice.

'When you first begin to meditate you should not expect too much too soon. The first day you start studying a foreign language you don't expect to speak it, do you?

'But even after only several weeks of practicing meditation you will begin to have more energy, and be a little bit happier. Gradually, as your meditation practice improves, you will experience even greater happiness and have more internal energy at your disposal. Eventually, as you further improve your meditation practice, you will experience ecstasy and knowledge that is beyond the power of words to describe!

'Each time you meditate, you create a stronger connection with the world of inner light and happiness that exists within you,' Master Fwap explained. 'Over the course of many years of practice, that connection will become brighter and more ecstatic. But even from the very beginning of your meditation practice, you will notice that some of the brightness and ecstasy

91

you experience during meditation will enter into your day-to-day life.

'Remember,' Master Fwap said in a mock tone of warning, 'as your meditation practice improves from month to month, more and more light and ecstasy will spill over into the moments of your daily life. Eventually a time will come when you will always exist, as I do, in a state of continual light.'

'Master Fwap, if all you learn from a master are the secret meditation techniques, why would you need to continue to study with a master once you have learned the techniques from him?' I inquired.

'You will need correction, direction, and most of all you will need your master's auric empowerment.' Master Fwap quickly explained.

'If you have electricity in the wires of your house,' he continued, 'you only have to plug a lamp in to make it work. The current is already there for you to use.

'But if you only have a small hand-powered generator to light a lamp, then you will only have light when you turn the crank of the hand generator. When you stop, the light will fade and go out.

'An enlightened master is a perpetual source of the cosmic light because his mind is always merged with nirvana. If you are a student of an enlightened master, then you can literally tap into his aura – the field of light that comes through him – anywhere and at anytime. All you have to do is meditate on your Buddhist master and the light will come into your mind.

'An enlightened Buddhist master provides his students with auric empowerment. He literally transfers light, power and knowledge into their auras. This empowerment gives his students an extraordinary amount of prana. This increased amount of prana enables them to meditate more deeply, and to accomplish other things in their lives more rapidly and with greater happiness and ease.

'Naturally, this is not the case for most people who meditate,' he continued. 'In this whole world, there are actually very few people who study meditation with an enlightened master. That is because there are not very many enlightened masters on the entire earth.

'Most people don't have enlightened masters,' he said with a slight sigh, as if the fact troubled him, 'so they only experience a limited amount of light when they practice meditation. But a person who wants to progress more rapidly and wishes to overcome unhappiness sooner, should try to find an enlightened master. If a person is serious about not just being a little bit happier, and if that person wants to become enlightened and experience infinite happiness, then he or she must study with an enlightened master. No one on this earth attains enlightenment anymore without an enlightened master as a guide . . . unless, of course, that person was enlightened in many previous incarnations.'

Master Fwap paused and looked directly into my eyes. The golden light was still filling the air between us. I felt my awareness change, and I simultaneously felt a strange tingling sensation at the top of my head. After staring into my eyes for several minutes, he resumed speaking.

'Nirvana, enlightenment, these terms are interchangeable. Call it anything that you want to: its nature is perfect harmony, peace and joy. Unlike the transient days of our lives that constantly come and go, nirvana has always been, is now, and always will be.

'This is the hardest thing in the universe to understand,' he said with a happy laugh. 'You must look beyond my words in order to know what I am talking about. You need to experience the reality of light yourself in your own meditation; only then will you really understand how perfect life is. Then, of course, you will be happy forever.'

'But Master Fwap! How can a person be happy in a world in which there is so much injustice and unhappiness? Everyone and everything dies! And there is so much pain and useless suffering in everyone's lives. How can meditation and enlightenment change all of that?'

'I agree with you,' Master Fwap said warmly. 'The world of human experience is very uncertain. Today you will be happy and then tomorrow you will be unhappy. Today you may get what you want and tomorrow you may not. Today you are young and filled with energy, and in the future you will grow old, and may become very tired.

'Only the enlightened are consistently happy, because their happiness is not predicated upon the events and experiences that take place in this world. Instead it is based upon the boundless inner energy they gain from their connection with the world of enlightenment.'

ॐ

Master Fwap Defines Astral Travel

'Beyond this world are countless dimensions. They stretch on forever! You can travel to them and have experiences in them.

'Some astral dimensions are bright and filled with ecstasy. Advanced cosmic beings live in them. But there are also very dark astral dimensions that are filled with pain and confusion. They are often inhabited by beings that are filled with hate and despair.

'The experiences that you have in astral dimensions are not essentially all that different from the experiences you have here in the physical dimension, in the sense that they are also transient. Some people make the mistake of assuming that it is always better somewhere else. But life is more or less the same wherever you go – because wherever you go, there you are.

'I mention this to you only because so many people seem to confuse the experience of meditation and enlightenment with astral travel. Some people travel to other dimensions in their astral bodies when they meditate. But astral travelling doesn't bring a person lasting happiness. As a matter of fact, if astral travelling is not done properly, it can be quite dangerous!

'It is an adversarial world outside of the safety of nirvana and enlightenment. In life, all beings need to feed on other beings just in order to exist. Some beings also like to cause others to needlessly suffer, just out of pure maliciousness.

'Just because you go to another dimension doesn't mean that things will be happier or better there for you. Actually things may be much more difficult.

'There are many different forms of life in the universe,' Master Fwap continued, with a tone of warning in his voice, 'and human beings are unaware of most of them. As you know, one small virus can take away your physical life. And as you have also learned, there are dangerous people and situations in life that you need to avoid simply to go on living, let alone to achieve happiness and perfect enlightenment.

'It has taken many years of your life just for you to learn how to successfully negotiate many of the physical dangers of the day-to-day world. Learning to cross a street in traffic, or turning down unacceptable or suspicious invitations from strangers are things you do that you now take for granted. But when you were first born, you didn't know about these dangers and how to deal with them. You learned about them from your parents, your teachers at school, and through other experiences you have had.

'Human beings only recently discovered that bacteria and viruses exist. I can personally assure you, as a Buddhist monk who has studied the riddles of existence for many, many thousands of incarnations, that there are also many other complex beings and life forms that inhabit other dimensions. They can be very dangerous when encountered, unless, of course, you know how to handle or avoid them.

'The point I am making is that enlightenment is not interdimensional travel!' Master Fwap said in a strong tone. 'Enlightenment is the experience of pure light. I have nothing against interdimensional travel; as a matter of fact, I do it frequently. But I learned to do it safely and correctly from my master, Fwaz Shastra-Dup.'

'What is interdimensional travel like?' I asked. Master Fwap had finally brought up a topic that sounded intriguing to me.

'Interdimensional travel is similar to travelling from one country to another,' he replied. 'Sometimes it is refreshing and elevating, and sometimes it is tiring and dangerous. But it certainly should not be confused with the experience of nirvana and enlightenment. Unlike the experience of nirvana, travelling to other dimensions will not take you beyond suffering, nor will it help you to experience the limitless ecstasy of creation. As a matter of fact, interdimensional travel has nothing to do with enlightenment at all.

An Enlightening Cup of Tea

'If you are enlightened you can experience ecstasy in any dimension and at any time!' Master Fwap exclaimed. 'Enlightenment is not related to where your physical or astral body may be, or to any experiences that you may be having with them. Enlightenment is beyond dimensionality. If it wasn't, it wouldn't provide permanent liberation from sorrow. It would only be another transient experience that eventually would culminate in sorrow as all other human experiences eventually do.

'That is why enlightenment is really worth seeking!' Master Fwap stated emphatically. 'It is the only thing that gives you permanent happiness. When you experience the ecstasy, peace and perfection of the endless and formless light of enlightenment, everything is all right. You are happy and free; you know life.

'Once you are enlightened, you can do whatever you want without fear or sorrow. You can choose to have a career or live in a monastery; you can go snowboarding, get married, stay single, be rich and famous or live unknown in a high Himalayan cave. It is up to you.

'When your mind is flooded with the pure light of nirvana, which is happiness itself, you will be delighted with whatever occurs to you.

'But without enlightenment, everything in life is harsh. Sooner or later you see everyone that you love die, unless you die first, of course. This causes you to suffer.

'But when you are enlightened, you see and understand that nothing and no one really dies,' Master Fwap continued. 'At the moment of death, a being simply changes forms. When you are enlightened, you know that everything and everyone, including yourself, is eternal.

'Armed with this knowledge, you no longer fear death or feel as much sorrow when those you love die. Once you have personally experienced enlightenment, you will see beyond the ocean of death to the everlasting shores of immortality.

'When you are enlightened and have united your mind with the deepest and most ancient part of the mind of the universe, you are not affected by suffering the way other people are. Naturally, your physical body will still feel pain if you get hurt, but you will not be overwhelmed even by extreme physical pain, because your mind will be filled with light, love and understanding.'

Master Fwap paused and closed his eyes. As he did, the golden light that filled the air between us suddenly became more solid. I couldn't see Master Fwap, or anything else in the room for that matter. It was as if I had joined Master Fwap in a dimension of solid gold light: nothing seemed to matter to me anymore. My mind had an unbroken continuity with all of creation. I was at peace.

Then Master Fwap spoke to me. It seemed as if his voice came from afar. At first I was only vaguely aware that he was speaking. Then I became fully aware of what he was saying to me.

'Because of your karma from your past lives, you will become enlightened in this lifetime. You have been enlightened in a number of your previous lives. You cannot avoid becoming enlightened. It will come to you when you are twenty-nine.

'But first you must prepare yourself. You must learn to meditate and stop your thoughts. You must overcome all egotism and selfishness by serving others. You must cleanse your mind so that enlightenment will find a happy place to reside there!'

ॐ

I listened to what Master Fwap said that day about enlightenment. His words touched something very deep within me. I knew, after he had spoken, that what mattered most in life was to be as aware as he was – to be enlightened.

I don't think I consciously understood most of what he said to me that day. But as he talked, I could sense the light and the wisdom that was behind his words. Somehow I could feel that he was in touch with the most perfect part of existence, and that was enough for me.

His reference to my future didn't really have much of an effect on me. He was talking about how I had been in past lives that I couldn't remember, and about what was going to happen to me in a future that hadn't yet occurred. I heard his words, but I don't think I particularly believed them, nor did I disbelieve them. Saying I was enlightened in the past and that I would be enlightened again in the future was something for which I simply didn't have any reference point. It was simply out of my league.

Master Fwap's reflections upon enlightenment, the visible golden light I had seen around him, and the way it had transported my mind into a world of perfect feelings, emotions and understandings, did affect me quite profoundly that day. Without my knowing how or why, I simply 'knew' what he had told me was true.

Master Fwap answered a few more questions I had about enlightenment, and then suddenly it was sunset. Somehow, without my noticing it, the golden light had vanished from the room and the two of us were sitting together in silence. The tea had grown cold.

ॐ

Master Fwap left me at the entrance to his temple and I walked back to the hostel along the narrow streets of Katmandu. As I walked, everything I saw seemed to glow and give off wave-like vibrations of light, not as bright as the light I had witnessed around Master Fwap, but more subtle and subdued.

Looking at the buildings as I passed by them, I could see they were really made up of dancing particles of energy. I now knew that the world wasn't really as solid as it looked.

Walking along the cold dark streets of Katmandu, I didn't feel very physical. Instead, I felt as if I was pure motion, a feeling I have experienced both before and since, when, on rare occasions, I have been snowboarding without any self-consciousness.

I slept well that night and dreamt of snow falling in the Himalayas.

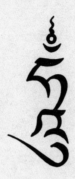

CHAPTER TWELVE

You Are the Board

ॐ

I didn't see Master Fwap for the rest of the week. During that time I reflected on our conversations about enlightenment, while I hiked up and snowboarded down ice- and snow-covered Himalayan peaks. Each morning I would hitch a ride to the mountains and climb up a snow-covered pass. Then I would snowboard down the mountain, climb back up, and do it again.

When I had said good-bye to Master Fwap at his temple door, he hadn't indicated where or when we would meet again, but I knew somehow that we would. I decided to stick to my snowboarding and leave the when and where of our next encounter up to him.

Six days after our parting, I unexpectedly met him again on the top of a mountain. That day I had spent three hours climbing up a particularly gnarly pass in search of perfect snow. After reaching the top of the pass, I had collapsed in a heap of exhaustion.

As I lay on my back in the cold snow, heavily breathing the thin mountain air in and out of my lungs, I closed my eyes and listened to the pounding of my heart. Then, quite unexpectedly, I felt a presence, as if someone was staring at me. I opened my eyes, and much to my amazement, Master Fwap was standing right above me! He was looking down at me with a big 'I know something you don't know' smile on his face.

Noiselessly, he sat down next to me. I lay on top of the snow-covered mountain peak, panting from exhaustion, breathlessly unable to convey my amazement at our unexpected meeting. A few minutes later, after I had finally caught my breath. I voiced my surprise.

'Master Fwap! What are you doing up here? Of all the possible mountains in the Himalayas, how could you have known that I would be on top of this one? When did you get here? Did you follow me up, or were you already here?'

'I have been waiting for you for a little over an hour,' Master Fwap quickly replied. 'Since this is a just-right mountain for this day, and since I have just-right karma, I knew that you would show up here!'

Before I could interrupt and ask more questions, he continued. 'Today I am going to teach you the art of living correctly. To live correctly, naturally you have to act correctly. Living is acting and acting is living. When the two become one, your life will be perfect.

'The Rae Chorze-Fwaz method of learning to live correctly is through the perfection of all your actions. If you can perfect any one thing that you do, then you will experience and know what perfect living is, in that particular action. Once you have accomplished the perfection of one particular action, it will then be relatively easy for you to transfer that knowledge to some other actions you perform, and eventually you will be able to perfect everything you do.

'It really doesn't matter which action I teach you to perfect first,' he continued. 'Any action will do, since the basic principles involved for perfecting any one action are the same for all actions.

'I have decided to teach you to perfect the action that you enjoy most,' he said with a mischievous smile on his face. 'I have come up to the top of this peak today to teach you how to go down this mountain on your snowboard perfectly.'

Master Fwap had trapped me and I knew it. While reincarnation and the secret doctrines of a Tantric Buddhist Mystery School didn't really matter very much to me, snow-boarding did. Snowboarding was everything to me. As unlikely as it seemed that Master Fwap could teach me how to snowboard perfectly, I decided right then and there that if he could, I would definitely become his disciple.

I immediately sat up and paid attention. I didn't want to miss a word he said.

'To do something perfectly, you must not think about what you are doing at all,' he stated in a strong and formal tone. 'Your thoughts are what create imperfections in your actions. They alienate you from the true reality of any action you perform.

'Thoughts should have a place in your life, of course, but it should be a very small place. To really know something, in order to see its perfection and to become part of that perfection, you must become the action that you seek to perfect.

'This will not be hard for you to understand if you look at any one of your actions. For example, you go down the mountain riding through the snow on your board. Your progression through the snow depends upon both your skill in using your board and your knowledge of the mountain and its snow. If you know what your board will do on different types of snow, and on different types of terrain, and if you and your board are "one," you will perform this action of going down the mountain on your snowboard perfectly.'

'But I already know how to do that, Master Fwap! I'm sure there is much more to learn, but so far I have been able to successfully snowboard down every mountain that I have ever tried.'

'Yes, you are accomplished,' Master Fwap responded. 'I have been watching you without your knowledge for the past several days. Yes, it is true. You are quite accomplished, but you are still far from perfecting your snowboarding.'

I respected Master Fwap's thoughts, and I really didn't mind the idea that he had been spying on me for the past several days – although I wasn't sure if I believed that he really had been watching me – but I still didn't see how he could be in a position to teach me how to snowboard perfectly. Since he wasn't an experienced snowboarder himself, I silently reasoned, how could he possibly know more about snowboarding than I did?

Master Fwap must have been reading my thoughts because he immediately addressed my concerns. 'You are wondering how I can show you how to do something perfectly, when you are the expert and I am the novice. There are two reasons: the first is that I am enlightened, and the second is that I know the principles of perfect action.

'Because I am enlightened, I can directly see the essence of anything I choose,' he said with a happy laugh. 'I can know its perfection with just a little bit of study. Additionally, since I know the principles of perfect action in other activities, I can transfer those principles to snowboarding or any other activity I choose.

'Let me show you,' he continued. 'May I borrow your board?'

I handed Master Fwap my snowboard. I didn't under-stand how he was going to use it, since he didn't have the proper boots. Master Fwap didn't seem to care. He stepped onto my snowboard and, giving himself a little push in the snow with his right foot to get started, he began his descent down the mountain.

I was sure that once Master Fwap started down the mountain and saw the severity of the slope that lay ahead of him, he would hop off my snowboard. We were on top of a Himalayan mountain. The slope was almost completely vertical. I wasn't even sure if I could safely make it down this particular mountain. With all the experience I had at my command, if I was unsure about snowboarding down this particular mountain, how could Master Fwap possibly do it and survive? I turned and watched nervously as Master Fwap rode my snowboard over the edge of the peak and began his perilous journey straight down the mountain's slope!

I kept expecting Master Fwap to hop off the board. But there, already several hundred feet below me, was Master Fwap, riding my snowboard perfectly and gracefully down the mountain without even the right boots to help him.

I had never seen anything like it in my life! He rode my snowboard as if he had been doing it for years. His form was perfect. I found myself laughing out loud as I watched him masterfully cut in and out of the deep powder.

About halfway down the mountain, Master Fwap took a very high jump and he and my board shot straight off the mountain. At first I thought there was no way he could survive the jump. He had gone straight out over a precipice, and there was nothing but several thousand feet of very thin air between himself and the icy ridge that lay below him.

For a moment he just hung in the air, suspended by the momentum from his jump. I knew that in only a few seconds gravity would change his trajectory, and he would fall to his certain death on the rocky ridge below!

And then the most incredible thing happened. Master Fwap and my board started to rise up in the air and come back up the mountain!

I watched dumbfounded as he flew through the air straight back up to the top of the mountain where I was standing. He was levitating! It was incredible. I didn't fully believe my eyes until he returned to the summit and was standing right next to me, calmly handing me back my snowboard.

'Master Fwap!' I exclaimed. 'How did you do that?'

'It was easy,' he replied with a slight smile. 'I simply became one with the board. I became the board. That is how I was able to go down the mountain without falling.'

'Yes, that was amazing,' I admitted, 'and your form was perfect. But that's not what I meant. How did you fly through the air and get back up here? You levitated. How did you do that?'

'Oh, that,' he replied, without any sense of pride or accomplishment in his voice. 'A little more complicated to explain, I'm afraid. My master, Fwaz Shastra-Dup, taught me how to do it, but it requires many years of effort to perfect the technique. It was a useful way for Buddhist masters to travel great distances before the invention of the automobile and aircraft. But these days it is much easier to drive a car or to buy a ticket and fly on a plane than it is to learn how to travel that way,' he said with a hearty laugh.

'I am afraid that in the modern world it is no longer worth the effort to learn the technique. But it is impressive when you see it for the first time, isn't it?'

'Yes.' I replied, still dumbfounded by what I had just witnessed.

'Master Fwap, would you teach me how to do that?'

'I could,' he replied, 'but as I said before, it takes many years to perfect the technique. It is much easier to travel the modern way. Now I travel mostly by car or plane.'

'But Master Fwap!' I protested. 'It would be very useful for snowboarding the Himalayas and other inaccessible mountains. I spend half the day just hiking up the mountain in order to get a fifteen-to twenty-minute ride down!'

'The exercise is good for you,' he responded with a broad smile and another laugh. 'And as I said, it is no longer worth the effort involved to learn the technique. But while I won't teach you how to levitate today, I will show you how to accomplish an action perfectly. I just did all of this to show you that I am qualified to teach you snowboarding. Did I convince you?'

He paused and looked at me seriously for a moment. I didn't know what to say at first. Then I replied: 'But of course you did; I'm convinced. But do I have to shave my head and put on an ochre-colored robe in order to learn from you?'

'No, definitely not!' he exclaimed. 'I'm afraid my Buddhist method of dress is not appropriate for a Western student of Tantric Buddhist Yoga.

'It is best for you to dress naturally, the way you currently do, and keep your hair any way you like. I am afraid that the significance of the traditional Buddhist way of appearing would not have a positive effect for you in your Western culture. It would be misunderstood, and you would be laughed at and made fun of.'

'What is the cultural significance of your appearance to someone who grew up here in the Far East, Master Fwap?'

'It is difficult to explain to someone who has not grown up in a Buddhist or Hindu society,' he replied. 'Let me just say that the Buddhist manner of dress and appearance creates respect for anyone who is a monk. It is well understood by members of my society that monks or masters are not ordinary persons. They have chosen to do a very difficult thing – to follow the pathway to enlightenment.

'In my culture the brightest and the most adventuresome youths have traditionally taken this path. Here in the Far East, studying yoga is comparable to a mixture of attending one of your best Western universities, like Harvard or Oxford, and of being an intrepid explorer, like one of your astronauts who travels into the faraway, unexplored regions of outer space.

'In the Far East, it is taken for granted that the training of a monk is physically rigorous and academically challenging,' Master Fwap continued to explain. 'As a monk, you learn to totally develop your mind, overcome all fears, be spontaneous and creative and most importantly, you learn to be able to go into unknown dimensions of the mind, and successfully return both ennobled and humbled by your journeys into the center of the universe.

'Dressing in the traditional Buddhist way would not transmit respect to you in the West. In the West, Buddhist monks are thought of as oddities. Most Westerners believe we are the remnants of an impoverished Third World society, upholding beliefs that have been outmoded by contemporary science. That is, I am afraid, the stereotypical view of the Far Eastern monk: he has a shaved head, wears an ochre robe, and is no longer relevant to the contemporary world. That is the view as seen through round Western eyes.

'For you, it is better to dress the way you do now and practice your yoga. In your society people are impressed by Ph.D. degrees, money and fame. I recommend that you attain all three and diligently practice your yoga. Then someday, when you teach our ancient practices of yoga to Western youths, you will be respected and admired. Then, because you will be wealthy, famous and have a Ph.D., the young students in the West will listen to what you have to say about Tantric Buddhist Yoga with great interest.'

I didn't know what to say in response to Master Fwap's remarks. I hadn't even decided whether or not I wanted to go to college, let alone get a Ph.D. I also thought that my chances of becoming rich and famous were pretty small, unless snowboarding suddenly became an Olympic sport, and I could endorse athletic products or something. I waited in silence for him to resume our conversation about snowboarding.

'The secret to doing anything perfectly is to practice and to become,' Master Fwap continued. 'That is all that there is to it, really. You must practice to learn about something. You must practice to get a feeling, a sense of the range of possibilities and the possible experiences that something can afford you.

'To a certain degree, you have already accomplished this with your board. But what you have not learned so far is how to become and to be. That is the next step in your inner education.

'You still see yourself as being separate from your actions,' Master Fwap explained. 'This, however, is untrue. If you could see inwardly through your third eye, the way I can, then you would know that inwardly you are "one" with all things, all actions, inactions, and all spheres of possible being.'

'Nirvana – enlightenment – is all there really is. Its power is everywhere and in everything. Your eyes cannot see it, your ears cannot hear it, your nose cannot smell it, your tongue cannot taste it, your body cannot grasp and feel it, but it is there, nevertheless. Nirvana and enlightenment exist just on the other side of your sensory perceptions and your thoughts.

'To do something perfectly, you must hook yourself to the power of the second attention and nirvana,' Master Fwap said. 'Once you can do that, almost nothing is impossible, whether it is levitating, snowboarding perfectly, or being enlightened.

'You come to know all of this through meditating,' he continued. 'In meditation, when your thoughts are stopped, you become empty. When you are empty, your mind folds back on itself and you see through the illusions of the material world.

'Things are not always as they appear! The world you see around you appears to be solid. But in reality, as any physicist will tell you, the physical world is made of moving energy. All matter is energy.'

'But Master Fwap!' I protested, 'I still don't understand any of this! How can you break a physical law like you just did when you flew up the mountain?'

Master Fwap laughed in response and grinned at me. 'It is because I have the knowledge of the nonphysical dimensions at my disposal. I step in and out of those dimensions, and use them to do things here in this world that would otherwise be impossible.

'The astral dimensions – when you have been properly instructed by a master in how to enter them, leave them, and deal with them – afford you opportunities to have experiences and gain insights into the structural nature of how dimensions are made up and phased together. The astral is the supporting ground for the physical dimension.

'Your understanding of the astral dimensions,' Master Fwap continued in a formal tone, as if he were presenting a paper before a scientific committee, 'can help you alter structures in the physical dimensions. It is in and through the medium of the astral dimensions that all of the siddha powers function and work.

'You can move in and through the astral worlds once you have gained control of your subtle body,' he said with tremendous energy. 'Remember, the astral worlds are the back corridors of eternity!

'Beyond the astral dimensions are the causal dimensions,' Master Fwap continued. 'The causal dimensions are not spatial or time-oriented. They are the planes of light, and they make up the outer limits of nirvana. Your experiences in the causal dimensions will give you the knowledge of time, space, dimensionality and what lies beyond all of these things.

'Remember,' Master Fwap said in summation, 'that what I am doing today is simply providing you with a verbal blueprint of how the universe works. At best it is a mere sketch of reality. Since what we are discussing is almost impossible to explain in words, at first my explanations may sound overly theoretical to you. It is like listening to a university professor discuss quantum mechanics. At first it can be confusing, and you may not see what all the theory you are learning has to do with actual physical applications.

'But be aware that a blueprint of a building is only a sketch on paper; it is not the building itself. Yet a blueprint provides a necessary template for construction. And, of course, when the actual building is finished, we throw the blueprint away.

'So in practical terms,' Master Fwap continued, 'if you wish to perform snowboarding perfectly, then you must turn it into perfect yoga. This is what I call mindfulness. It is the direct application of Tantric Buddhist teachings to a physical event, a way of doing or accomplishing something, or a way of thinking and viewing something.

'Tantric Yoga is not simply sitting and being absorbed in meditation,' Master Fwap said with sudden emphasis. 'While formal meditation is certainly a critical part of Tantric Buddhism, Tantric Yoga is also a process of turning all of the activities and experiences of your daily life into meditation.'

'Master Fwap, please correct me if I am wrong. But what you are saying is that you are going to teach me about enlightenment by showing me how to snowboard perfectly. Is that right?'

'Yes,' he quickly replied, 'it is. But to snowboard perfectly, you also must know how to meditate well.'

'So is there an interrelationship between meditation and physical events? Or is meditation just sitting there and spacing out on enlightened bliss?' I inquired.

'Yes and no!' Master Fwap replied, laughing. 'Meditation is the ability to be in a state of perfect mind. At the same time, it is the ability to do physical things in a harmonious way; it is a way to remain centered in a physical world that is out of balance.

'In Tantric Buddhism we learn to meditate in two ways. First we learn how to sit and focus on our

114

chakras and stop our thoughts. Then, when the mind is empty, we can travel into the astral dimensions, the causal dimensions, or if we are very advanced in the practice of meditation, we can merge our minds with nirvana itself.

'The second way we learn to meditate in Tantric Buddhism is by practicing mindfulness,' he explained. 'Mindfulness is the practice of doing physical things perfectly – in a state of emptiness – in which we become consciously "one" with whatever physical or mental activity we are currently engaged in.

'You will find that as you gain more control in your meditation,' Master Fwap said, 'it will be much easier for you to practice mindfulness. You will also find, conversely, that the practice of mindfulness – of doing physical and mental things perfectly – will help you improve your daily meditation practice.

'In practical terms, what all this means,' Master Fwap concluded, 'is that when you come to know that you are the board, your snowboarding will be perfect. But as long as you conceive of yourself as being separate from your snowboard, of riding on top of your board, or of directing your board, then this will not be true.

'When you seek to direct your board,' he said, 'you are creating an unnecessary conceptual separation between yourself and your snowboard. The result will be that your actions are awkward and imperfect. But if you *are* the board, then you – the board – will direct yourself perfectly. You – the board – will know best, what it is that you can and cannot do.'

Master Fwap shifted his position slightly on the snow. 'Most people make a mistake in life: they *think* their lives instead of *living* their lives. They believe that what they do, who they are, and how they do what they do, is something they must think about and choose. This

115

way of approaching life, however, doesn't create perfect actions. As a matter of fact, this approach to life makes a person very egotistical. People who *think* their lives instead of living them directly, automatically assume they always know the best way of doing everything.

'But when we come to see that we *are* the thing that we do,' Master Fwap continued, 'then we will be directed by the doing of that thing rather than egotistically attempting to imperfectly direct our own emotions.'

I must have looked somewhat confused because Master Fwap laughed good-naturedly and paused for a moment before resuming his explanation.

'When, for example, you are on your snowboard going down a mountain, you must decide how to direct your board. But whether you are aware of it or not, your board has an inherent knowledge of its own capabilities because it is made up of intelligent energy, just as you are.

'In Tantric Buddhism,' he continued, 'we call the inherent knowledge that all animate and inanimate objects possess of themselves, their "emptiness." It is the Buddhist belief that all things, experiences and people are inherently empty. That is simply a way of saying that all physical and nonphysical things have another side, a side that is not visible to the senses or accessible to the reasoning mind, a side that can only be known and experienced intuitively by emptying one's own mind of thoughts, judgments and predispositions about life and how it works.

'Normally,' Master Fwap explained, 'we only acquaint ourselves with the physical side of something. We come to know it as we choose. But to be honest with you, the physical side of a person, an animal, a plant, a thing or a place is minute in comparison to its nonphysical side.

'Take me, for example!' Master Fwap's voice resonated. 'You can see my physical body with your eyes. But my physical body is nothing in comparison to my nonphysical body.

'My nonphysical body is the part of myself that lives forever. It is ancient and complicated. It has lived through countless lives in both this and in other worlds.

'It knows things and can do things that you cannot possibly imagine. But if you look at me with your eyes, you will only see my physical side, and you may underestimate me!

'When I travelled back up the mountain on your snowboard a few minutes ago, you were very impressed. I did that with my nonphysical body – with my subtle body – with my essential emptiness.

'Try always to remember that when you think about something, you separate yourself from it. But when you are empty – when your mind is tranquil and at peace with the universe, when it has become void of all thought – you become meditation. Then you consciously join with and become part of the power that is in everything around you.

'Everything knows what is best for itself!' Master Fwap exclaimed. 'That is what the Sanskrit word "dharma" means. Dharma means the best of all possible actions.'

I must have looked a little bit bewildered again, because he paused and asked me if I understood what he had just explained. I acknowledged my confusion, and then he was silent for several minutes. Then he spoke to me again, at a slower pace.

'Let me sum all of this up for you,' he began. 'If we think and try to direct our lives with only our limited, rationalistic thoughts and our sense perceptions, then our actions and our activities will not be perfect. From a Buddhist perspective, it is incorrect to always assume that we know what is best.

'When we take the time to meditate and empty ourselves of thoughts, we immediately connect with the inherent emptiness of our actions and experiences. When we do this, our nonphysical side merges with the nonphysical side of that which we are experiencing.

'Once this has occurred, our actions and experiences will direct us. In other words, we will be guided by the inherent emptiness of the things we choose to interact with.

'One day, when you have learned to meditate well enough, you will come to see that in the state of emptiness, you are the action, not the performer of the action. Remember, always allow the action of an activity or an event to take precedence over your own point of view. This is the Tantric Buddhist way. Allow the emptiness inherent within actions and experiences to guide and shape your choices. Let your actions direct you, the actor, not the other way around.

'Before beginning an activity,' Master Fwap instructed me, 'always first empty yourself of thoughts regarding what you are about to do. Then allow the inherent emptiness within what you are about to do to direct you. Instead of your ego directing you and making countless mistakes, allow yourself to be guided by the invisible principles of the universe within your actions. At that time there will be a perfect flow of energy in whatever you choose to do, and there will be a grace and power present in all of your movements. From a Tantric Buddhist perspective, this is perfect action.'

Master Fwap paused again for several minutes, giving me time to reflect on his explanation. Then he spoke again.

'Now you will go on your board down the mountain.

But first you must make your mind still. Then allow the emptiness within your board to guide you. Let it become your will. Remember, you *are* the board! Then your ride down the mountain will be perfect action. Try it.'

I thanked Master Fwap for his discourse on emptiness and perfect action, and got onto my board. 'Perfect action,' I thought to myself. Then I closed my eyes and tried to empty my mind of all thought. For some reason it was easy to do on the top of that Himalayan peak. Suddenly I was flooded with energy and I could feel the power – what Master Fwap had been calling the emptiness of the mountain – flowing through me. I had no thoughts and yet I was completely aware.

I opened my eyes and let go to my snowboard. It was me and I was it. I glided down the mountain, cutting back and forth through the granular powder without any conscious effort on my part. It was exactly as Master Fwap had described: my board and the mountain knew better than I did how to interact. I just let them take over and I enjoyed the ride down. It was the most perfect run I had ever made down a mountain.

When I got to the bottom of the mountain, Master Fwap was waiting there for me with an 'I told you so' smile on his face. Without talking, the two of us walked down the road together.

CHAPTER THIRTEEN

Tales of Powder

ॐ

I spent the next several days by myself, snowboarding the Himalayas, practicing Master Fwap's 'emptiness method' for perfecting my technique. It took some experimentation, but after a number of runs down the mountain I gradually began to get the sense that I was part of my snowboard, and that my snowboard was an extension of myself. My snowboarding rapidly improved.

While I experienced some of the most wonderful moments of my life during those few days, I also noticed that at times I was incredibly lonely.

Loneliness has never been a very precise feeling for me. Whenever I have felt lonely, I haven't felt that I missed anyone in particular. It has always been more of a vague feeling of uncertainty, a poignant and unfulfilled longing for an undefinable condition, other than that which I was experiencing at the time.

I usually started to feel lonely each day about an hour or two before sunset. The feeling would always come upon me quite unexpectedly, and it didn't seem to be predicated upon or triggered by any particular phenomena.

I may have been snowboarding happily for hours, when quite suddenly this feeling would sneak up on me. Often it was followed by or accompanied with additional feelings of frustration or despair.

It always began in the same way: I would notice that I wasn't smiling anymore. Then, as it grew stronger, I would begin to feel somewhat disconnected from what was happening around me, or from what I was physically doing at the time. I usually attributed these feelings to physical exhaustion and high altitude. But I noticed that these emotions would always enter my mind at around the same time each day when I was in the mountains, regardless of how much sleep I had gotten the night before.

I had grown accustomed to feeling this way while snowboarding in the late afternoons in North America, but I noticed the feelings of loneliness that I experienced in the hour or two prior to sunset were even more pronounced when I was snowboarding the Himalayas.

During the early part of the day I would very much enjoy being alone while I snowboarded. But in the late afternoon, usually around the time I was making my last run down a mountain, I would find myself feeling what I had come to refer to as 'cosmic loneliness.'

I had nicknamed the feeling cosmic loneliness because the emotions that I felt at these times had an almost spatial dimension to them. On the particular occasions when these feelings were most intense, I felt as if my mental perceptions extended beyond my body and this world to something infinitely more powerful, and that my personal concerns were overshadowed by what I could best describe as these 'otherworldly' feelings.

ॐ

In the late afternoon in the Himalayas, the cloud cover would usually thicken and the sky would turn fantastic shades of pink, magenta, soft rose and lavender. At these moments of incredible physical beauty, I would often be standing on the top of a lone peak looking out over the snow-rimmed mountain horizon. Instead of being filled with exaltation by all of the beauty that lay before me, I was often filled with an unbearable feeling of emptiness and despair.

The emptiness that I felt at these times was not the happy and ecstatic emptiness that Master Fwap had described to me. Often the sheer weight of those feelings would cause me to feel insignificant and lost. My gut reaction at times like these was to 'beat feet' back to the hostel in Katmandu and find a pretty girl to laugh and spend some time with.

I had the chance to ask Master Fwap about the incongruity of these feelings several days later. On that particular day, I had spent a happy morning snowboarding down yet another nameless Himalayan mountain. The powder that day was fresh and deep and I had made a wonderful series of runs. I had climbed back up the mountain for my last run of the day when, to my utter amazement, I saw Master Fwap waiting for me on the top of the peak.

'Master Fwap!' I blurted out. 'What are you doing here?'

'I have come out here to visit you,' he replied with a broad smile. 'Since you were not content to be with a beautiful girl in one of the many scenic restaurants in Katmandu today – as most young men your age would be – I found it necessary to come out here to

123

the top of this particular mountain to engage you in conversation.'

'Master Fwap,' I inquired wistfully, 'why is it that I often feel so lonely at this time of day? I don't really have any reason to. Where does this feeling of loneliness come from? I know this might sound a little crazy, but somehow it doesn't quite feel like it is even my own feeling.'

With a quick movement of his right hand, Master Fwap brushed the snow off an adjacent rock and sat down on it. I sat down next to him on my snowboard and made myself comfortable. He didn't say anything for several minutes and I assumed he was considering my question. Suddenly he began to speak.

'There are many things to understand in life,' he began. 'And as you are beginning to find out, things are not always as they appear to be. Take different times of day, for example. It would seem that there shouldn't be any significant difference between different times of the day, don't you think? It would appear to be logical that all times of the day would be approximately the same.

'The numbers that human beings have assigned to the hours of the day,' Master Fwap continued to explain, 'and the names they have given to the different times of day, such as morning, afternoon, sunset, evening, late night and sunrise are, after all, only words. Since time itself appears to be relatively uniform, other than the names and numbers that have been applied to these different periods, there really shouldn't be any difference in the quality of time itself throughout the day.'

'But Master Fwap,' I interrupted, 'people do different things at different times of the day. Most people get up in the morning, work or go to school during the afternoon, and sleep or party at night.'

'Yes, that's true,' he replied with a knowing smile.

'But there are also other people who work at night and sleep during the day. So other than the activities people participate in at different times of the day or night, during the absence or presence of daylight, you would assume that the actual substance of time throughout the day would be uniform, wouldn't you?'

'Yes,' I replied, 'I would.'

'Most people would agree with you,' he said with a broad smile. 'But the truth of the matter is that the quality of time actually changes throughout the day and night. Behind the visible world that you see in front of you each day, there are many invisible dimensions. A great number of these dimensions interconnect with our physical world.

'Some of these dimensions are place-specific,' Master Fwap explained. 'In other words, they only touch certain geographical areas. Other dimensions are more time-specific, in that they only interact with the physical dimension they touch during specific times of the day or night.

'During the late afternoon and early evening – starting from about two hours before sunset and ending at approximately two hours after sunset – there is a specific dimension that interconnects with our physical world. This particular dimension can best be visualized as a series of horizontally shaped geometric planes that extend from wherever you may happen to be at that time of day, on out into infinity.'

'But Master Fwap, how can that be? Since the time of the sunset is constantly changing locations on the earth during a twenty-four hour period, does that mean that this dimension is constantly circling the globe? And why would it be connected to a specific time of day? Times of day are caused by the turning of the earth in relation to the sun. Why would that have anything to do with the shifting of a different dimension?'

Master Fwap smiled at me and laughed lightheartedly. I could tell that he was getting a kick out of my scientifically based Western logic. He paused for a few moments and closed his eyes. Then, without opening them, as if he was deeply concentrating on something, he began to speak again.

'Life is magic! You need to accept this as a basic premise in any conversation we have about Tantric Buddhism, and the Buddhist view of the universe. Science tries to understand and explain the physical magic of life with theorems and experiments. We, as Buddhists, do the same thing, only we use theorems and do our experiments to explain and understand the nonphysical side of life.

'But whether it's Buddhism or science trying to explain the universe to us,' he continued, 'life – in its essence – ultimately remains magical and inexplicable.'

'What do you mean when you say that life is magic, Master Fwap?'

'I mean that it cannot be completely explained or logically understood. I know that it is popular in this era to believe there is a logical explanation for just about anything and everything that exists or happens. Since we Buddhists are reasonable people, we would also like to believe that everything that occurs in other dimensions, as well as in this dimension, can be explained through reason and logic.

'But the truth of the matter is, many aspects of life cannot be explained through logic or reason. The reasoning part of the mind simply doesn't have the capacity to understand many of the whys and hows of being and nonbeing.

'While the thinking and reasoning aspect of our minds

may not be able to fully understand certain sides of life,' Master Fwap continued, 'we do have another hidden part of our minds that can. In Buddhism we refer to this hidden part of our understanding as the intuitive or higher mind.

'The intuitive mind is nonphysical,' Master Fwap said precisely, as if he wanted me to pay particular attention to this concept. 'It is not part of the brain or any other cellular structure in the physical body. It is part of the causal body.

'As I mentioned to you before,' he continued, 'the causal body is the part of a person that lives forever. It is what you would call the soul. It doesn't dissolve along with the physical and astral bodies at the time of physical death, at the end of an incarnation.

'The causal body is the most ancient and timeless part of a person. It has the capacity to know and do things that the physical mind and body cannot.

'Perhaps it will be easier for you to understand what I am talking about if I give you a concrete example,' Master Fwap said with a subtle smile. 'The most concrete thing in the universe is matter. As I am sure you are aware, learned scientists can explain quite a bit about matter. They know that it is formed of different elements, and that those elements are composed of specific atomic and subatomic structures. But while matter can be analyzed and its structures understood, scientists will never be able to understand why matter exists in the first place.

'It is the same in Buddhism. Buddhists who practice occultism, which is the scientific branch of Buddhism, seek to understand and explore the chemistries of time, space, dimensionality and awareness.

'While the study of occultism enables those who study it to attain an understanding about how dimensions work the way they do, what consciousness is made up of, how the different states of mind interconnect with each other, how to move between them, and many other things, it still cannot reveal to us why consciousness and dimensions exist in the first place.'

'So then, what good is occultism, Master Fwap?' I was beginning to feel both cold and frustrated. I was sitting on the frozen snow and the late afternoon temperature was dropping rapidly. I felt a definite chill. Master Fwap's explanation wasn't clarifying anything about my feelings of cosmic loneliness. From my point of view, he was only further confusing the issue by discussing things that didn't even seem to be in the least bit relevant to my original question.

Master Fwap must have understood my frustration. 'Be patient with me,' he said. 'I first have to give you a little background information, to help create a perspective from which you should be able to understand my answer to your question.

'You, like most people your age, want to know everything all at once. I admire your enthusiasm. But to be honest with you, as I must be since I am a Buddhist monk, most of the important things that we learn about and experience in life can't be understood immediately. Some things take a lifetime, if not several lifetimes, to fully grasp.

'For example, let us consider how the movement of a nonphysical dimension creates the feeling that you describe as "cosmic loneliness," which you experience in the late afternoons and early evenings in the mountains.

'What you call loneliness, I call power!' Master Fwap said sharply. 'Since I have studied Buddhist occultism to an extent, I can tell you that in the late afternoon, the dimensions of power become more manifest and accessible to us.

'Because you are psychic, you can feel those dimensions,' he said, suddenly looking directly into my eyes, 'even though you may not be aware of the true nature of what you are feeling, and of the opportunities that those particular dimensions of power can afford you.

'I know about these things,' he continued, 'because my own master, Fwaz Shastra-Dup, explained them to me, and also because I have validated the things that he taught me with my own research and life experiences.

'You are innately psychic because you have meditated and practiced yoga in many of your past lives,' Master Fwap stated matter-of-factly. 'You were born this way into this life because of your past-life development. But since you grew up in a non-Buddhist culture, there was no one to explain these things to you when you were a child, or to show you how to develop and understand your innate psychic talents, as you matured from childhood into adolescence and young adulthood.

'Since you are more psychic than most other people, you can feel things that they cannot. You can feel when the dimensions shift at different times of the day. But because you do not understand what you are feeling, and how to work with and gain power and higher awareness from those feelings, you are somewhat confused and alienated by them.

'The feeling you describe as cosmic loneliness,' Master Fwap continued patiently, 'is your emotional reaction to the intensity of the dimensions of power that are present in the late afternoon. These particular dimensions of power are often perceived as being spatially immense. It feels like they go on forever and ever, and in a way they do.

'Your instinctive reaction to the perception of that immensity is to feel dwarfed by it. Since you have not made friends with that immensity, as I have, and since you have not understood its beneficial side, you tend to react to these dimensions of power by feeling small, insignificant, overwhelmed and alienated.

'It is as if you are confronting the totality and immensity of the universe,' he continued. 'You feel as if that immensity out there is about to crush you and destroy your identity. Your reaction is to run for cover and seek something familiar – like a familiar location and the company of others you like or trust – to shut out those overwhelming feelings. Once you have managed to do that, you feel safe. You can forget about that immensity out there and feel secure in your identity, and with familiar circumstances again.

'But what you fail to see and understand,' Master Fwap said very softly, 'is the incredible beauty and the majestic power that these particular dimensional planes can make available to you in the late afternoons and early evenings. Some day, when you come to see and understand these things, you will be able to access the power and beauty of those dimensions and bring them into your own life.'

'How can I come to see this, Master Fwap?'

'Sometimes we react to things that we don't understand with fear, misunderstanding and confusion. The alternative to this type of reaction is to cultivate a healthy curiosity toward things, situations and feelings that we don't understand, and to react to them with curiosity instead of with fear.

'There are invisible powers and forces behind everything in life!' Master Fwap suddenly said in a loud voice. 'Usually we react to these powers and forces with disbelief, prejudice and violence, or we can choose to have a more enlightened view toward things that we don't immediately understand.

'It is good to have a healthy curiosity about the

unknown that is not based on fear,' Master Fwap said with a broad smile, 'just as it is equally important not to have an irrational need to believe in things that may not be true, simply because we feel the need to rationalize the things in life that we don't understand.

'It is the Tantric Buddhist belief that the visible universe is a kind of revolving doorway that can take us back and forth between the invisible dimensions,' he continued.

'Many of the invisible dimensions afford us magnificent and breathtaking views of the universe. Other dimensions can empower us, elevate our ability to perceive, and give us knowledge about our past lives. And still other dimensions can help us to be happier and more successful.

'Human beings usually train their young to run away from things that they don't understand. It is an old bad habit. They teach their children to hide from, rationalize and be unduly afraid of, death, the immensity of life, and the experiences of the spirit.

'When human beings live this way, they shut out both the high and low frequencies in their lives. This leaves them with the boring midrange experiences in daily living that they perceive to be safe. In this way, the world of human experiences is reduced to a world of feeding, toiling for a living, reproducing and continuously fending off the unknown.

'But some of us are born with a different karma!' he happily exclaimed. 'We cannot be content to experience only the mundane aspects of life! We need to feel both the high and low-range frequencies of existence, because all of the frequencies of existence that we see in the external world correspond to different frequencies within ourselves.

'Everything that you see around you exists somewhere

inside of your mind. Your mind contains all of the frequencies of life in seed form. We experience feelings of wellness and happiness when we allow ourselves to freely and intelligently experience all of the higher frequencies of life. We become unhappy, depressed, self-destructive and needlessly violent towards ourselves and others when we experience too many of the low range vibrations of life.

'Life is a delicate balance between the magical forces of creation and the magical forces of destruction,' Master Fwap continued. 'The primary reason that most human beings are so unhappy is that they cut themselves off from the more complex and beautiful tonal ranges of existence. To be truly happy we need to experience, balance and create a synthesis between the high, midrange, and lower frequencies that life affords us.

'Most people blame their unhappiness on the elements of their lives,' Master Fwap said sympathetically. 'If they are unfulfilled, they assume it is because they don't have the right job, enough money or the right sexual partner. They believe that if the universe would only conform to their desires, and would give them everything they want, then they would be happy.

'But human beings cannot be happy, whether rich, poor or at any point in between, if they have cut themselves off from the magic of creation. Contemporary human beings have explained away the meaning of life with science and logic – without explaining anything at all! And what they have not been able to explain away, they have chosen either to ignore, or to file away as being unimportant or irrelevant.

'Whenever a society chooses to ignore what it perceives as the incongruities or uncomfortable aspects of life, you will notice that problems with sexual obsession and violence often occur. Our failure to deal in a more positive and insightful way with any part of the life process is, more often than not, a sign of psychological and spiritual neurosis.

'All of life is holy!' Master Fwap shouted happily. 'There is no such thing as sin. There is only ignorance, and that can easily be cured with inner knowledge.

'The Buddhist view is to not be afraid of the immensity and the magic of life!' he continued in a celebratory voice. 'This is where Tantric Buddhism varies from the traditions of most human societies. In our practices we accept everything. We enjoy and learn from the physical sciences, the arts, and also from the vast panorama of human experiences. In addition to enjoying and learning from all of these physical things,' he continued, 'we also consciously explore the spiritual dimensions within ourselves and the universe.

'Don't seek to hide from the immensity of what you feel at sunset,' he counseled me. 'Explore it and learn from it. Instead of simply labeling the feelings you experience at that time of day as "bad" and "uncomfortable," merge your mind with them and become one with them.

'The great Buddhist teachers of the past have developed safe, effective and refined methods of meditation for moving our minds into the astral and causal dimensions. Once you have learned the Order's secret meditation methods, you can explore any dimensional plane with your mind without fear or prejudice.

'Through the twin practices of meditation and mindfulness,' Master Fwap continued to elaborate, 'you can safely learn to experience all of the different vibratory ranges in the universe. Eventually you will learn to combine and recombine these frequencies within your own mind. The endless combinations and recombinations that these frequencies can create are part of the infinite number of ecstasies that enlightened Buddhist masters experience every day.'

ॐ

Interdimensional Snowstorms

I asked Master Fwap if he would explain, in more physical terms, the high and low-range 'frequencies' he had mentioned to me. I thought I understood some of what he had said to me, but parts of his explanation still seemed difficult, if not impossible, for me to grasp.

'Master Fwap, would you please tell me a little more about these high and low-range frequencies?'

'Yes, of course. But first let me recite a mantra that sums up all of this. It is our Tibetan theory of relativity. Einstein expressed his theory of relativity as an equation. He said, "$E=mc^2$."

'In Tibet we say it slightly differently. We say "Om Mani Padme Hum."'

'What does that mean, Master Fwap?'

'It means that enlightenment exists within all things. That is the Tibetan theory of relativity.

'Everything that exists outside of us also exists within us,' Master Fwap declared. 'This is one of the great mysteries of life! Enlightenment, which is the essence and the nexus of infinity and eternity, exists right here and now, within your own mind and heart.

'As I have told you before, enlightenment is inexpressible; it cannot be shared in words. Terms may be used to try to express what enlightenment is like, but none of them are absolute.

'Naturally, enlightenment can be alluded to. I can say that it is the highest ecstasy, the most perfect happiness, the deepest experience of peace, and all that is good and perfect in life. But that is only a way of talking, a way of beating around the bush, because none of the descriptions of enlightenment – no matter how simple, complex or elegant they may be – can cause you to experience it.

'However, while words may not be able to transmit the experience of enlightenment, they are useful for explaining some of the meditation techniques and methods that are used for gaining the experience of enlightenment.'

'Master Fwap, I still don't see what all of this has to do with the different feelings that I experience in my life. I also don't understand how enlightenment and all of the countless dimensions that you say exist can be both inside and outside of me at the same time.'

'Yes, yes,' he replied. 'I was just getting to that.' He shifted his position on the rock he was sitting on, and suddenly sat up very straight. 'The high and low frequencies that I was alluding to are the countless dimensional planes of light and darkness that exist both within and outside of us. There is a perfect interrelationship between the inner and the outer worlds. They correspond to each other.

'As I told you before, life is a mystery,' he continued. 'I cannot explain why this is so, any more than I can explain to you why the sun is in the sky, or why we, or any of this, exists in the first place. I am simply pointing out some things to you that I have experienced and come to know through Tantric Buddhist practice; things that you may be unaware of.

'But in order for you to fully understand the frequencies of life,' Master Fwap remarked, 'you must first understand that all existence is made up of vibrating, intelligent light.

'There are many types of inner and outer light, and they vibrate at different frequencies,' he explained. 'The faster the vibration of light, the more ecstatic it is to experience.

'The real trick in life,' Master Fwap stated, 'is to consciously alter your vibratory frequency, to speed it up! Each of us is born with a specific vibratory rate. You might say we are each intelligent energy that vibrates at a specific speed.

'Each of us is born as a particular pattern of energy,' Master Fwap said firmly. 'The pattern that each of us is, has been modified and added to, by the experiences we had in our past lives.

'Why each of us is the particular energy pattern that we are is a mystery. It cannot be known here. All I know is that we have always existed as this pattern, and we always will. Our pattern can be modified, but it can never be completely changed.'

'Why is that, Master Fwap?'

'The whys of life are not the concern of the practitioners of Buddhist Yoga. They are the concerns of philosophers. Practitioners of Buddhist Yoga are interested in how the universe works; they study the intricacies of its structures, and with the knowledge that they gain from their studies, they are able to have direct experiences of ecstasy and enlightenment that are far above the intellectual abstractions of philosophers.

'A chemist doesn't know why an atom exists. It isn't the chemist's job to know. What he or she does know about is how atomic and subatomic structures come together to create molecules and elements, and how varying combinations of elements can create new substances or alter old substances.

'In a similar way, a Buddhist Yoga master doesn't know why the universe works the way it does; he knows how it works the way that it does. With this knowledge he can turn any experience or situation, no matter how obscure, difficult or painful, into something positive and enlightening!'

'Master Fwap, perhaps you cannot explain "why" the energy pattern that is ourselves exists, but can you at least tell me a little bit more about it?'

Master Fwap smiled at me quizzically and replied, 'In Buddhist Yoga we classify the different patterns of energy that sentient beings have as soul types. An almost endless array of vibratory soul types make up the beings that populate the universes and dimensions. The particular vibratory rate of a specific soul type is what causes it to incarnate within a specific universe and also within a specific body type.'

'So in other words, Master Fwap, the types of souls that dogs have would be similar to each other, and the types of souls that human beings have would also be similar to each other, at least in terms of their vibratory frequencies. But the soul types of dogs and of people are very different. Is that right?'

'Yes,' he replied. 'You have it exactly right. Dogs

are one specific soul type, human beings are another soul type. There are also much more subtle differences between the types of souls that different breeds of dogs have, and for that matter there are differences between the soul types of dogs within a particular breed.'

Suddenly I began to get excited. I thought I was catching on. 'So then, Master Fwap, that means that the differences in the soul types within Terriers, for example, wouldn't be as great as the difference between a German Shepherd and a Chihuahua, is that right?'

'Precisely!' he replied. He was smiling at me as if I had finally said something correctly. 'And all the soul types that incarnate in a particular dimension are somewhat similar!

'But to reincarnate in another dimension,' he explained, taking the conversation to a deeper level, 'it is necessary for a being to radically repattern itself by significantly altering its vibratory rate, whereas to make lateral shifts within a dimension that a soul is reincarnating in, doesn't require as radical a repatterning of the soul's basic vibratory rate.'

'Master Fwap, I used to have a girlfriend who was very interested in reincarnation. She told me that every soul, when it is first created out of the cosmic flux, starts out in a basic form, like a rock, and that eventually, through the process of reincarnating in millions of lives, it moves forward and experiences being a plant, then an animal, and finally it incarnates as a person.

'She said that in each kingdom into which a soul incarnates – mineral, plant, animal and human – it starts at the bottom of the evolutionary ladder, and gradually, through the process of reincarnation, works its way up to the top. Once it reaches the highest level of evolution that is possible within a specific kingdom, the soul then moves on and starts reincarnating again at the bottom level of the next higher evolutionary kingdom.

'She compared it to getting your first job at a company, working on the production line, and then, throughout the course of your life, working your way up the corporate ladder, until you eventually became the president of the corporation. She said that every soul does that, and that eventually every soul reaches enlightenment. Does reincarnation really work that way?'

'Not entirely,' he replied. 'I know this is a very common explanation of the process of reincarnation, but to be honest with you, it is much too simplistic. I believe that your girlfriend was referring to the commonly held theory that each soul begins its cosmic journey by reincarnating in the simplest forms of life. Then, according to this theory, each soul takes subsequently more advanced incarnations in different bodies, always moving toward higher stages of evolution. Eventually, every soul reaches the highest levels of incarnation, becomes enlightened, and dissolves back into nirvana. That is probably the theory she was alluding to.'

'But if that's not how it really is, then how does it work, Master Fwap?'

'Normally we start out as a specific soul type, and we remain in that soul type forever,' he replied. 'We evolve as that soul type, but we don't ever change soul types; we just develop the soul type that we have.'

Now I was confused. He had lost me again. 'Master Fwap, I don't understand! Why would we stay in the same soul type forever? Why shouldn't we evolve through the process of reincarnation, and all eventually become enlightened?'

'Because we get used to being who we are, and we are drawn back repeatedly to reincarnate in the dimension we have become accustomed to,' he replied with a hearty laugh. 'Our soul type is our basic structure,' Master Fwap continued, 'and it becomes very familiar to us. It is very hard for us to change it because – in order to do so – we literally have to erase the multilife being who we have gotten used to being. That is why so few souls in the cosmos ever become enlightened. They become attached to the soul type that they are, and also to the dimension in which they reincarnate.'

'Master Fwap, now I am totally confused,' I said in exasperation. 'I thought everyone became enlightened once they had gone through enough incarnations. That is what my girlfriend told me.'

'No,' he responded with a cherubic smile and a soft chuckle, 'it is not usually so. And now, if you will permit me, I will confuse you a little more!'

Master Fwap didn't say anything for several minutes. He seemed to be collecting his thoughts, or perhaps he was creating a sense of drama by pausing before his next revelation.

'My young friend,' he finally began, 'there has never been a time in which you and I have not existed, nor will there ever be a time when we will not be.

'This is not only the case for ourselves, but for all of the sentient beings that exist in all of the far-flung universes that comprise eternity.

'Think of life as a snowstorm. As far as the eye can see, there is nothing but beautiful white falling snow. In my analogy, each soul is like a snowflake in the endless white snowstorm of infinity.

'The winds of karma,' he continued,' blow each soul back and forth, from one life to another, within the same endlessly white interdimensional snowstorm.

'For a brief moment we are alive in this world, and then the winds of our karma change direction, and we

140

are blown into yet another life, in another part of the same storm.

'Almost all souls stay within the same soul typing,' he continued. 'Naturally they will evolve and devolve from lifetime to lifetime, speeding up and slowing down their basic vibratory rates, according to the actions that they perform and the thought forms they hold, in each of the incarnations they pass through.

'But on rare occasions there are souls that consciously redirect and repattern themselves, and change their soul types, while their deepest essence remains the same. If they have the knowledge, power and inclination to do so, they can change soul types at will, many, many times, as they pass through the endless interdimensional snowstorms of eternity.

'In order to become enlightened,' Master Fwap explained, 'it is necessary for a soul to repattern itself thousands of times. This is what advanced Buddhist Yoga is really all about. It is the science of repatterning the soul within an incarnate body, and also in the bardo planes, which the soul passes through in between incarnations.

'If you learn and practice the science of repatterning, then you can literally change your soul type within your current body structure. If you did this during your current incarnation, then naturally, at the time of your death, your soul would change inclination and you would reincarnate in a different dimension. You would then be with soul types that were similar to the new soul type you had just repatterned yourself to be.

'Let me sum this up for you,' Master Fwap said with a serious look on his face. 'Very few beings become enlightened. By that I mean that very few souls have the inclination, knowledge and power to overcome their attachment to their multilife form and to the dimension they have incarnated in for so long. To become enlightened, a soul must transcend its attachment to its familiar form and dimension, and go through a series of repatternings, over the course of tens of thousands of incarnations, until that soul finally incarnates in an enlightened soul type. Then, once it has incarnated in the form of an enlightened soul type, it must go through the training and discipline of evolving even further beyond that soul type to becoming nirvana, which, of course, is beyond soul types and repatterning.

'Try to understand,' he said, looking concerned, 'that it is not better to be an enlightened soul type, or to attain enlightenment for that matter, than it is to do or be anything else! It is a personal choice that the essence of our being makes for reasons that cannot be known here.

'What does matter,' he continued, 'is getting to the high end of the spectrum of the soul type and dimension that you are currently incarnating in. Then you will be happy. Becoming enlightened isn't everything, because enlightenment is everything.

'All souls are, in their essence, enlightened,' he continued to explain. 'Just as one of your body's cells contains the DNA of your entire species within it, so too within each soul, regardless of its soul type, there is a spiritual type of DNA. Within this spiritual DNA is enlightenment! The goal of life and of reincarnation is not to become enlightened – but simply to be and to live life fully, and to have endless experiences in eternity.

'You may be drawn to the experience of enlightenment. If that is the case, then you will learn to repattern yourself in an upward ascension of vibratory soul types. If that is your fate it is both challenging and happy, because unlike most beings, you will eventually experience nirvana directly, and as a result you will gain the knowledge, and experience the ecstasy that is beyond expression.

'In an interdimensional snowstorm, one snowflake does not have a better journey than another snowflake does. They are simply different. Souls group together according to their vibratory rate. That is why those souls that seek enlightenment associate with and are drawn to similar souls, and are even more drawn to enlightened souls who can teach them the art of repatterning.'

I had become so involved in listening to Master Fwap's explanation of reincarnation that I hadn't even noticed that the sun was beginning to set. I suddenly realized that I was freezing cold.

At that moment it occurred to me that I still had to snowboard down the mountain before it became any colder and darker. I knew it would be fully dark before long, and I wasn't sure that even if I left immediately, I would be able to make it all the way down. In my thoughts I imagined that I would be trapped on the mountain in the freezing Himalayan night.

'Don't worry,' Master Fwap said, as if he were reading my thoughts. 'I will ride down with you on your board and help guide you.'

And so the two of us held on to each other as we sped down the mountain, cutting rapidly in and out of the deep powder, on my small four-and-a-half-foot-long snowboard – two snowflakes, blowing through eternity in an endless interdimensional snowstorm.

CHAPTER FOURTEEN

Hierarchical Versus Relational Snowboarding

ॐ

Master Fwap and I had spent most of the late morning and afternoon climbing up a steep, rock-strewn mountain pass. The terrain was difficult but spectacular. We stopped to rest at the top of the pass. I estimated that we were at around eighteen thousand feet. I could barely breathe.

I lay back on the ground listening to my lungs sucking in the cold mountain air and to the loud pounding of my heart. Looking up, I noticed that Master Fwap had assumed a cross-legged position, was sitting up very straight, and had closed his eyes. His breathing was calm and regular. His face was serene. An aura of sparkling golden light surrounded his head and shoulders.

After a few minutes, my breathing began to normalize. A sharp wind had kicked up, bringing a cold chill with it. I sat up and zipped my parka, which I had unzipped only minutes before while climbing because I had felt so hot.

There was hardly any noise to be heard anywhere.

The only audible sound was the soft whine of the wind rushing up and down the canyons of snow. Smoky gray storm clouds that had drifted in from the northwest had started to filter out some of the sun's light and warmth. I was about to ask Master Fwap if he thought a storm was coming when, unexpectedly, he opened his eyes and directed his gaze toward me.

'At this time of year,' Master Fwap began, speaking in a very measured way, 'snow showers can come up quite unexpectedly. I shouldn't worry, though. I know where there is a cave just on the other side of this pass.'

After a few more minutes, we both stood up and started walking down the trail. The scenery that greeted my eyes as we traversed the mountain was breathtaking. Immediately below us, the mountain descended into a deep valley filled with a rhododendron forest. A steamy, smoke-like haze hung over the tops of the huge rhododendrons, almost shielding them from sight. If the fog hadn't parted momentarily, the valley below me would have been completely obscured by clouds. I thought that this would have been a suitable location for the legendary lost civilization of Shangri-la.

As I looked out beyond the valley, the Himalayas seemed to stretch on forever. Mountains of endless snow melted into each other as far as I could see. The pure whiteness of the scene was occasionally broken by dark mountain crags so windswept that all the snow had been blown off their peaks, revealing the stark black rock beneath.

We descended for about an hour and a half, walking carefully on the slippery, snow-covered ground. About halfway down to the rhododendron forest, we made an abrupt left turn off of the trail we had been walking on, and started walking down a smaller path.

The path wound around the mountain toward the

south. After about ten minutes Master Fwap stopped walking and paused, apparently to take his bearings. Then we started walking again.

In a matter of minutes, we came to the mouth of a large cave. The opening was about fifteen feet high. Beyond the mouth of the cave there was only blackness. Master Fwap gestured for me to follow him in, and walking carefully in his footsteps I entered the cave.

After we had walked about thirty steps into the cave, Master Fwap stopped. He told me to turn around and sit down next to him on his right. As soon as I turned around, I could see again. Some of the outside light was reflected back into the cave by snow that had formed in a ledge around the cave's mouth.

Sitting down, I noticed that we were resting on solid rock. The snow didn't seem to have drifted very far into the cave. I was surprised by how warm it was inside the cave. I realized that most of the cold I had been feeling prior to entering the cave was not the real air temperature, but was caused by the Himalayan wind chill factor.

We sat in silence for several minutes before Master Fwap spoke to me. Sitting in the cave, I felt a familiar feeling. Usually after a long day of snowboarding, after I have packed up my gear and the sun has begun to set, I look up at the mountains that I have been snowboarding all day long, and I experience an exquisite sense of peace and well-being. I feel relaxed and happy, and nothing else really matters much. That was exactly how I felt while sitting next to Master Fwap in the Himalayan cave that afternoon.

'There are many caves like this one in the Himalayas,' Master Fwap began. 'These are the hermitages of the great Buddhist masters of our Order. Members of the Rae Chorze-Fwaz have been meditating in caves like these for thousands of years.

'These caves are places of power. They are located along interdimensional power lines and energy vortexes. Because of the dimensions they intersect with, it is very easy to meditate here and to understand concepts that might otherwise be difficult, if not impossible, to grasp in other locations.

'Many of the universities in your country are similarly placed,' he said in a matter-of-fact way. 'They are built on locations that intersect with dimensions of great clarity. Teaching and learning in locations of that type naturally is much easier. If the same university were placed just a few miles away on a different site, without the proper interdimensional openings for clarity and learning, it would be much harder for the students to learn there.

'In life, location is everything. We know a little bit more about this in the Far East than you do in the West!

'Most of the time, when the officers of a Far Eastern corporation find a prospective location for their corporate headquarters,' Master Fwap continued, 'they hire a Taoist priest who specializes in interdimensional openings to check out the proposed site. If he feels the location for the corporation is not appropriate – from an energy flow perspective – then he will recommend that the corporation not build there, and the company will choose a new location.

'A great deal of what you would call "success" in a person's life,' Master Fwap continued,' comes from the ability to choose the right location to do whatever it is that the person wants to do in life. There are "just right" spots for every type of activity, and there are also other spots that will make the same activities difficult, if not impossible, to perform or participate in successfully.

'There are physical locations on the earth where it is easier to meditate, to study, to learn, to make corporate decisions, to fight battles, and to see into other worlds.

What gives a physical location a particular type of power are the dimensional lines that run through it.

'Throughout the earth there are lines of power,' Master Fwap continued to explain. 'There are many different types of these astral lines and they carry different types of energy along them.

'Think of the earth as being superimposed on a grid of horizontal lines. Dimensional space and locations are superimposed over horizontal grids of light and energy. These grids are points of egress – points that open into other dimensional realities in which there is much more prana available.

'For instance,' Master Fwap asked, 'did you know that there are specific energy lines running through the earth that open up to artistic and musical dimensions? If a composer or an artist lives and works in a place that has those types of lines running through it, then it will be much easier for him to create great works of art or music. If the same composer or artist lived and worked in a place without those lines, his work would be much harder, and he probably wouldn't create much great art at all!

'While most people may not consciously know about energy lines, grid planes, interdimensional vortexes and how all this works, they unconsciously use their intuition, which I call the second attention, to find and use "just right' locations when they need them to achieve success.

'For example, when the site for a great university was originally chosen, the founding fathers often intuitively picked a "just right" spot for learning. Standing in that spot, even if it was only a forest or a meadow at the time, their bodies could "feel" that this would be a good place for students to learn. To be honest with you, people who are successful in life have at least unconsciously learned to use their second attention to choose the 'just right' spots they need to do their work in.

'Thousands of years ago, the members of the Rae Chorze-Fwaz roamed the Far East looking for the "just right" places to practice meditation and other psychic arts,' Master Fwap continued. 'They discovered many places of enlightenment, places of power, places of healing, places of seeing and places for teaching. Since these were their primary interests, these were the types of places they sought out and discovered.

'This particular cave is a place of seeing,' Master Fwap explained. 'It is easy to see other worlds and dimensions from here, and it is also easy to understand complicated occult concepts here. Naturally, once you have understood a difficult metaphysical concept here, that knowledge will accompany you when you leave this cave, in much the same way that you will retain a concept you have learned at school after you have left your school and gone home for the evening.'

At this point, I interrupted Master Fwap. He had aroused my curiosity, as I somehow suspected was his intention.

'Master Fwap,' I asked, after he had paused for a moment, 'is there a particular mountain that is better to snowboard on than any other mountain in the world?' I tried to make the tone of my question seem light and conversational, so he wouldn't suspect how much I really wanted to know the answer. Having travelled with Master Fwap now for some weeks, I had learned that his sense of humor was bigger than the Himalayas, and that if he even half suspected that I wanted to know something badly enough, he would deliberately not tell me, just to drive me crazy.

Master Fwap remained silent for several minutes, considering my question before responding. I assumed that, as usual, he was going to prolong my agony for as long as possible, milking the situation for all it was worth. He surprised me, however, with the directness of his answer.

'Yes,' he began, 'there is only one absolutely "just right" mountain for snowboarding in the world, although there are certainly many other mountains that are very good for snowboarding.'

'Where might that mountain be, Master Fwap?' I inquired as nonchalantly as possible, trying as best as I could to mask my rapidly increasing excitement.

'It is not very far from here,' he whispered. 'It is a special mountain. Its power is pure and exact. You would find it both the most challenging and enjoyable mountain to snowboard in all of the world.'

'When can we go there?' I asked a little too loudly. I could no longer conceal the excitement in my voice.

'On our last day together I will take you there,' he replied, again in a hushed tone of voice, as if he was imparting a most important secret to me and was concerned that someone else might overhear what he was saying.

'But that is still some time from now, and today we have other things to concern ourselves with,' he quietly said.

'What's on the agenda for today?' I asked with a sigh, trying my best to conceal my disappointment with the fact that he hadn't told me the location of the perfect snowboarding mountain. I immediately knew that there was no way I could leave the Himalayas and Master Fwap until I had snowboarded this 'perfect' mountain. Master Fwap had masterfully hooked me, and what I found to be most frustrating was that I had baited the hook myself!

'What is the most important aspect of snowboarding?' Master Fwap asked me.

'Balance,' I replied quickly.

'Exactly so!' he exclaimed. While I couldn't see his face in the semidarkness of the cave, I could tell by the tone of his voice that he was smiling.

'Balance is also the most important aspect of living. I say that it is the most important aspect of living as a way of focusing your attention on balance as a topic.

'Naturally every part of living is important!' he said in a much louder voice, having evidently decided to give up his pretense of secrecy. 'But without balance in your life nothing else will work,' he continued. 'Just as, in snowboarding, without balance you will fall over, in life, without balance you will never be happy or successful.

'Life is complicated,' Master Fwap explained. 'It is only simple on television or in the movies. But for purposes of this discussion, let us say that the goal of life is to be happy. It is the primary motivating force for the vast majority of human beings' actions and decisions; all other decisions and actions that people make are subordinate to this.

'You choose from among the experiences that life has to offer you,' he continued, 'those which you feel will make you the happiest. It's important to remember this. In snowboarding, the purpose is to glide down the mountain on your snowboard without falling off. If you lack balance then you won't be able to do this.

'In life, happiness is achieved through balance. Naturally, the kind of balance I'm discussing is inside of your mind. Certainly it's a good idea to try and create a happy balance in your physical life too,' he remarked. 'But because of the constant uncertainties and the ever-changing circumstances in day-to-day living, it is not always possible to achieve perfect physical balance in all of the activities in your life.

'It is important to try, though. Your efforts to create

a balance in the activities in your physical life will maximize your possibilities for achieving happiness.'

'What is inner balance, Master Fwap?' I inquired. 'To be honest with you, I really have no idea what you are referring to.'

'I appreciate your honesty. That is why I will give you an honest answer: inner balance is happiness.'

'But wait a minute!' I interjected hastily, 'I thought you just said that inner balance creates happiness. Now you are saying that inner balance is happiness. How can it be both? I don't understand!'

'Have patience, my young friend. Hardly anyone on this entire planet understands this point. That is why we have hiked all the way up to this cave, because here you may gain an understanding of what inner balance and happiness are, and how they can be attained. If we had this conversation elsewhere, I sincerely doubt you would understand very much of what I will explain to you today.'

'But Master Fwap!' I protested. 'How is it that only a few people on the entire earth, out of billions and billions of people who inhabit our planet, could understand this? I mean, aren't there lots of really happy people out there?'

'Not really. The only people who are truly happy all the time, no matter what the circumstances of their lives may be, are enlightened masters. And there are only a few of us still left on this earth.

'But you are right, in a sense,' he continued. 'There are certainly many people who do experience happiness from time to time. But their happiness is usually short-lived, because it is dependent upon the outer circumstances of their lives being in accord with the fulfillment of their desires.

'To understand this, you must first know the difference

between a hierarchical and a relational mind-set,' Master Fwap explained.

'Master Fwap, not only do I not know the difference between them, but I don't even know what they are. Would you please explain this to me in snowboarding terms?'

'Yes, of course, I would be most pleased to,' he replied.

ॐ

Master Fwap Explains Relational Snowboarding

'There are five basic ways to approach snowboarding, or anything else in your life for that matter,' Master Fwap began. 'There are also numerous combination approaches, which blend different elements of these five basic approaches.'

'What are they, Master Fwap?' I inquired.

'The first approach to snowboarding,' he began, 'is the instinctive method. This is the least effective of the five. Using this method, you allow your body's basic cellular instincts to guide you.'

'Which instincts do you mean?' I asked.

'Fear, pleasure and physical balance,' he quickly responded. 'You are willing to learn to snowboard, and go through what is necessary to do so, because your body anticipates a pleasurable experience from snowboarding. You use your body's fear to keep yourself from getting hurt, and you also use your body's innate sense of balance to stay on your board and negotiate going down the mountains of snow.

'The second method is the passionate approach. In this method, you use your desires to prompt you. In the passionate approach, your ego guides you and your passions empower you. This is the machismo method.'

'So you mean that you do it to show off?' I asked.

'Yes and no,' he replied. 'That is certainly an element in this approach, but there is more to it than that. In the passionate method, you are validating your self-image through your conquests and achievements in snowboarding. You will most certainly combine this with the instinctual approach. In your travels, you must have met other snowboarders who employ this method.'

'Sure I have,' I said with a grin. 'I call it the jock syndrome. Those guys snowboard just to prove to themselves, or to other people who are watching them, that they can be radical. It's very much an image thing. And a lot of them are very good snowboarders, too.'

'Exactly,' Master Fwap replied. 'They physically enjoy the feeling of snowboarding, and they use their fear, their sense of balance, and their ego's self-assertive need to achieve, in order to impress themselves and others. Their passions drive them to accomplish more than the purely instinctual snowboarder does.'

'Right!' I said. 'Guys and women like that like to swagger when they walk. They think they are better than other snowboarders are if they can pass them on the downhill. It's not really a spiritual thing for them, if you know what I mean.'

'Indeed I do,' he responded. 'Now, the third approach is the irrational way. It is not really a method at all. It is dominated by anger and uncontrolled aggression. People who use this approach will skip over the preliminary lessons and instruction about how to snowboard, and just do it! They will also probably end up in a hospital, or put someone they run down in the hospital along with them.'

'Right on, Master Fwap!' I agreed heartily. 'I hate those dudes! They are completely unfocused! They just grab a board and try going downhill. Every time they fall off they just get angrier. They usually end up quitting or getting themselves or somebody else hurt. They are bad news from start to finish. I don't even know why they bother.'

'They probably don't know why they're snowboarding either,' he said. 'But then again, that is how they choose to live their entire lives. They just grab onto anything they see, and with all their anger they try to make it work for themselves. When it doesn't, they blame it on someone or something else, but never on themselves. They live in a world of hate and blame.'

'I know what you mean, Master Fwap,' I said. 'I once saw one of those guys smash a snowboard to pieces when he couldn't ride it. He kept yelling that the board was no good. But the board was fine; he was his only real problem.'

'Now the two more evolved methods of snowboarding are the hierarchical and the relational methods,' Master Fwap explained. 'These two methods of snowboarding represent the Western and Eastern approaches to life and to problem solving. They are mental approaches, as opposed to the physical or emotional approaches of the previous three methods I outlined.

'Both the hierarchical and relational methods,' he continued, 'rely on the intelligent uses of structures. The primary difference between the two methods, however, is the way in which people who use them arrange, interrelate and put those structures to use. To understand these two methods, you have to know the difference between Buddhism and Christianity.'

'Why is that, Master Fwap?'

He laughed and said: 'It has to do with circles and

straight lines. These are respectively the symbols of the Orient and of the West.'

'What do circles and straight lines have to do with snowboarding?' I asked impatiently. I was getting the feeling that Master Fwap was about to launch into another one of his mystical dialogues, and that somehow the answer to my question was going to get buried in one of his metaphorical avalanches.

He chuckled at my impatient tone of voice and then, without losing any of his elegant Buddhist composure, continued with his explanation.

'Hierarchical and relational thinking are both extensions of religious viewpoints,' he said. 'While Buddhism is not as strictly practiced as it once was in the East, and Judaism and Christianity are also not practiced as strictly or widely as they once were in the West, the types of thinking that they respectively engendered in the Eastern and Western cultures remain relatively unchanged.

'Hierarchical thinking stems from the Christian belief in the great chain of being. In the Christian religious view, God is at the top of the universe and the devil is at the bottom. Everyone else exists at different levels, according to how divine or undivine they are, in between God and the devil. Dante, along with many other Christian writers, helped make the hierarchical view part of the mainstream of Western thought and philosophy.

'According to this Judeo-Christian hierarchical way of thinking,' Master Fwap continued, 'creation began at a specific point in time in the past, and the end of the world will occur at some specific point in time in the future.

'Everything is linear in this mind-set, and time and space occur in straight lines,' he continued. 'These two very basic concepts, along with the idea that man is born in a state of corruption and sin and is in need of redemption, created a physical and metaphysical cosmology that influenced the very structure of the Western peoples' languages, philosophies, methods of thought and analysis, problem solving and, of course, their social value systems.

'In other words, people in the West – unless they are irrational or intuitive – tend to think in straight lines. Let me give you a snowboarding example.

'A hierarchical snowboarder snowboards in a straight line,' Master Fwap explained. 'He begins at the top of the mountain and snowboards straight down it. When he reaches the bottom, he stops, and then he ascends the mountain again and repeats the process.'

'But Master Fwap,' I interrupted, 'how else can you snowboard down a mountain? You have to go with gravity, unless someone can levitate like you can.'

'Yes,' he replied. 'What you say is true. Unless you can levitate, this is most definitely the case. But you interrupted me before I had a chance to finish my explanation.

'As I was saying,' he continued, 'a hierarchical snowboarder thinks in a straight line. His method of accessing his snowboarding skills is linear.'

'What does that mean in practical terms?' I asked.

'Why, it means that the data constructs in his mind move fairly slowly, not a good thing for such a fast-moving sport, I would think.'

'Master Fwap!' I said with renewed exasperation. 'I don't have any idea at all what you are talking about! If this cave is supposed to make things more clear, it isn't working very well. Are you sure we are in the right location?'

'Hmm? Oh yes, thank you, I am quite sure. But you must be patient and let me finish. I am just getting to the practical part.

'You see,' he continued with what I hoped was a sympathetic chuckle for my frustration, 'it is hard to imagine

158

thinking in another mode when you have thought in a particular way all of your life. What we are really discussing is how we remember things, how we connect things within our mind, and how we prepare for and anticipate things.

'This is how your mind processes information. It connects ideas and feelings in a particular fashion, and then it sorts them into patterns and matches them. It can do so in and through either a hierarchical, relational or irrational framework.

'Relational thinking is based on circles,' Master Fwap continued. 'That is how Buddhists see the world, as a series of endlessly interconnected circles.

'We don't believe in God or in the devil, at least not as they are commonly conceived in the eyes of Westerners. We also don't believe that time is linear. Instead, we believe that God and the devil, good and evil, and all of the pairs of what you would call opposites, exist inside your own mind. And we don't feel that these things are opposites at all – as a matter of fact, we view them as complementary.

'As Buddhists we believe that time occurs in cycles, that the entire universe is one big circle, and that many smaller circles and cycles are contained within that larger circle.

'Needless to say, both the hierarchical and the relational cosmologies and views of life are slightly off the mark. They are both attempts to define existence in a way it really cannot be defined.

'As an enlightened Buddhist master, I am not concerned with cosmologies,' Master Fwap digressed for a moment, 'only with the effect that they have upon the way we think, and the way that we construe data.

'So, to answer your question,' he continued, 'a hierarchical snowboarder takes longer to think things through because he must connect all of his thoughts in straight lines. A relational snowboarder can think faster because he thinks in circles – that is, he doesn't have to go through as many time-consuming thoughts to make relevant connections between the things he thinks about and perceives!'

ॐ

Master Fwap Discusses Lines and Circles

'For example,' Master Fwap said, 'let us say that we have placed a great deal of information along a straight line. Now, if we are at one end of the straight line, and the piece of information we want to get to is all the way at the other end of the straight line, it will be necessary for us to journey all the way through the information that is in between us and the piece of information that we want to access, in order to reach it.

'But suppose we took the same data and arranged it along the circumference of a circle – and then let us further suppose that we sat down in the middle of that circle of data. Now, all of that information would be equidistant from us because it is arranged along the circumference of the circle that we are sitting in the middle of.

'If we want to get to a particular piece of information, we don't have to go through a lot of useless data to get to it. All we have to do is reach right out to the edge of the circle and grab it! Obviously this is a much quicker and more efficient way of accessing information.

'Take snowboarding, for example. Suppose . . .'

'Wait a minute, Master Fwap!' I interjected. 'You don't snowboard in circles!' As I made this statement, I felt very proud of myself. I felt that I had found a flaw in his Buddhist logic at long last!

'You are correct,' he replied. 'But although you may not snowboard in circles, you can think and perceive from the center of the circle.'

'What do you mean by that?' I asked.

'By not thinking at all,' he replied.

'But what good would not thinking do you, Master Fwap? If you weren't thinking when you were boarding down a mountain, you would probably end up killing yourself, wouldn't you?'

'Not at all. That is what relational thinking is all about. It is perceiving things from the still center inside of your mind. Normally your thoughts and perceptions are linear. You have to think things out in a long, cumbersome fashion in order to arrive at a proper conclusion.'

'But that's what deductive and inductive logic are all about!' I protested.

'That's exactly my point,' he continued, unfazed by my emotional outburst. 'Logic is a hierarchical way of thinking; whether it is deductive or inductive is irrelevant. It really boils down to the same thing.'

'What's that?' I asked hesitantly. I was getting more and more frustrated as he continued his explanation. I still didn't understand how any of this related to snowboarding.

'I see you're losing your patience with me again,' he replied. 'Well, this isn't really that hard to understand. Just assume that logical thought and reasoning normally move in a straight line.

161

'Say, for example,' he continued, 'that you are snow-boarding down a strange mountain, and suddenly a Buddhist monk appears directly in your path. Logically, thinking in a straight line, he shouldn't be there at all. What on earth would a Buddhist monk be doing wandering around in the snow on a Himalayan mountain?

'Instead of relationally thinking – with which you would have instantaneously reacted to the situation without logical analysis, and thus would have avoided hitting the monk – you hesitate for a split second because your logic cannot account quickly enough for his unexpected presence on the mountain.

'Now if you were thinking relationally, which would mean that you weren't thinking at all, your body would react instantly and you would avoid hitting the monk,' Master Fwap continued. 'Whether the monk's being there was logical or illogical wouldn't be an issue that you would have to think your way through, in order for you to react. You wouldn't lose that split second it takes to get through your logical analysis of the situation. You wouldn't hit him, and thus you would avoid all the bad karma that comes from snowboarding over an unsuspecting, enlightened Buddhist monk.'

Master Fwap paused. Even though I could not see his expression in the semidarkness of the cave, I was sure he had a self-satisfied grin on his face.

'Master Fwap, how is what you just described any different from instinctual reflexes? In what way is this relational? Also, isn't not thinking when you are snowboarding basically the same thing as being uncon-scious?'

ॐ

162

Master Fwap Defines The Center of the Circle

Before answering my question, Master Fwap was silent for several minutes. I assumed he was pondering how he was best going to answer my questions, or perhaps he was considering how he could simplify the subtleties of Buddhist wisdom for a rather abstruse American snowboarding fanatic.

'This is not as difficult to understand as it might seem at first to you,' he resumed. 'The main problem you are having is that you are being a little too serious . . . you need to relax your mind and let the luminous energy of this cave help you understand all of this.

'In short, you are paying much too much attention to my words and missing the yogic point that they are directing your mind toward.

'Imagine, if you will for a minute or two, a universe of data – an endless amount of data of all types – that stretches in all directions. While some of this data may be applicable to your immediate needs, most of it, at any given moment, is irrelevant. So the problem you are faced with, in a universe of endless data, is how to eliminate all of the data that is irrelevant or extraneous to your immediate needs, as rapidly and as effortlessly as possible, and instead to quickly find, focus on and employ the data that you do need to solve and fulfill your immediate problems and opportunities.

'One of the great secrets of life that Buddhist monks have learned from their study of meditation,' Master Fwap explained, 'is how to eliminate anything extraneous from their minds. If something doesn't contribute to their happiness and well-being, or to the happiness and well-being of others, they are able to remove it

163

from their thoughts and keep their minds focused on what does matter.

'While you are plummeting down the mountain on your snowboard, your mind normally would be thinking of many different things. You might be remembering something irrelevant, you might be anticipating something unnecessary, or you might be focusing your mind on exactly how you are doing what you are doing. For most people, at any given time, it is usually a mixture of all three of these things.

'The relational way of doing things is to move your mind to a fourth condition, a condition of heightened awareness. In a condition of heightened awareness, you elevate your conscious mind above the stream of extraneous data – out of dimensional time and space, so to speak – and you meld your mind instead with the pure intelligent consciousness of the universe.

'When your mind becomes absorbed in this higher level of intelligent consciousness – which I refer to as the second attention – your mind will automatically access and create new relations with the data that you require, at any given moment of your life. This is the center of the circle of intelligence! In this condition of inner illumination, you will always know exactly the right thing to do or not do, at exactly the right time! Unlike using a hierarchical mind-set, you won't have to think your way through a great deal of data to understand things. You will simply "know."

'Ultimately, thinking is a very inefficient method of processing data . . .'

'But Master Fwap!' I almost shouted in sheer frustration, 'You're not making any sense at all! I thought the shortest distance between any two points at any given time was a straight line.'

'Sometimes it is, and sometimes it isn't,' he calmly replied.

'Well, when isn't it?!!!' I nearly yelled out at the top of my voice in frustration.

ॐ

'Consider a road that goes up to the top of a mountain,' he calmly responded. 'It winds its way up to the top of the mountain in a series of loops. If you made a road that went straight to the top of a mountain, it would be too steep for vehicles to climb. So, in theory, while the shortest distance between two points may be a straight line, in reality, sometimes a circle, or a series of circles, is shorter.'

I didn't answer. I could understand now the benefits of the training in Buddhist debate that Master Fwap had received growing up in the monastery. I remained quiet, silently acknowledging his point, and let him continue.

'The issue we are examining,' Master Fwap continued, 'is about thinking relationally. As I said before, most people think in straight lines – when they bother to think at all. And naturally, you do understand, my young friend, I am certainly not suggesting that we all give up thinking and return to a purely instinctual way of perceiving things. My point is that there is a much more advanced way of looking at life than you are familiar with; it is a way of perceiving life and data that is much more accurate and enjoyable than the method of logical analysis which you are used to employing.

'Logical analysis,' Master Fwap continued, 'is fine for gaining a limited understanding of many things and situations. But the speed, accuracy and range of computations that it offers you – as a way of thinking over and evaluating real time experience and situations – is definitely inferior to relational analysis.

'Let me give you one more example, and perhaps all of this might become more clear to you. Do you have your flash-light with you?'

'Yes, I always carry it in my pack in case it gets dark on the way back from snowboarding.'

'Good, take it out for a moment, turn it on, and point it at the ground in front of us.'

After I had done as he requested, Master Fwap spoke again.

'Now suppose we take a set of numbers . . . let us arrange them in two rows. Let us arrange the first row like this,' he said as he drew this set of numbers in the snow:

$$1\ 2\ 3\ 4\ 5\ 6\ 7\ 8\ 9\ 10\ 11\ 12$$

'And suppose we draw a second set of numbers that looks like this,' he said. And he drew a second set of numbers, underneath the first set, that looked something like this:

$$1\ 2\ 3\ 4\ 5\ 6\ 7\ 8\ 9\ 10\ 11\ 12$$
$$13\ 14\ 15\ 16\ 17\ 18\ 19\ 20\ 21\ 22$$

'Now, logically speaking,' he went on, 'the best way to relate these numbers is in a straight line, either from side to side or up and down.' Then Master Fwap drew some lines in the snow between some of the numbers that he had written that looked something like this:

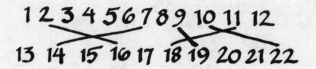

'But suppose we arranged the first group of these numbers in a circle instead,' he said as he made a circle out of the same numbers that looked something like this:

'And now let's make another circle using the second set of numbers, inside of the first circle,' he went on. And then he drew a second series of numbers in a smaller circle, that fit within his first circle, that ended up looking something like this:

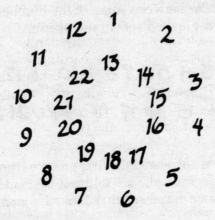

'Now, as you can see for yourself,' he continued, 'the ways of connecting the numbers are much more direct than before, when I was interconnecting the numbers that I had placed in the two straight lines.' And he proceeded to draw a number of lines connecting the numbers in the two circles that looked something like this:

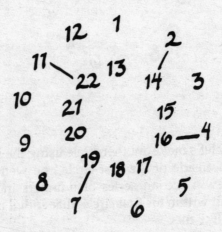

'You're right, Master Fwap,' I said. 'The lines connecting the numbers in the two circles are much shorter than the length of the lines connecting most of the numbers that are in the two straight rows. But what does this have to do with snowboarding?'

'It is our Buddhist belief,' he replied, 'that the human mind, as I once told you, is made up of countless layers – which I have represented with circles. Think of your mind as being similar to an onion.

'An onion is made of hundreds of layers of thin skin. When you take the outermost layer away, another layer is revealed. There is layer after layer, as you peel your way down to the onion's core.

'Your mind is made of thousands of layers in a similar way,' Master Fwap continued. 'That is why I compare it to a series of interconnected circles.'

'But Master Fwap!' I broke in. 'How does any of this relate to snowboarding?!!' I was completely exasperated at this point with all of Master Fwap's metaphysical jargon. I didn't see how any of what he was saying was at all relevant to answering my question.

'It's easy,' he said, suppressing a laugh as he spoke. 'I will explain it to you. Be patient with me for just a few more moments.'

'OK,' I acquiesced, 'but please relate it this time to snowboarding.'

'When you are thinking, you are caught in a straight line,' he began. 'In order to get out of the straight line of thought and reach a point of information that is not in the current straight line of your thoughts, you need to bridge your information gap with additional straight lines of thought.

'For example, let us suppose that you are snowboarding down a mountain. You are engaged in the types of thoughts that you normally think while you are snowboarding. Perhaps you are gauging the snowbank ahead and preparing to turn . . . when suddenly, and without warning, you see a Buddhist monk standing in the path of your rapidly descending snowboard.

'But if you are not thinking at all,' he continued, 'if your mind is absorbed in the second attention, and you are able to make extralogical connections within your mind with immediacy, then you will react smoothly to this unexpected occurrence and avoid hitting the poor unsuspecting Buddhist monk with your snowboard. If you are thinking in straight lines however – as you were when you first met me – then you would hit the monk, just as you did.

'You hit me,' Master Fwap continued, bringing me back mentally and emotionally to a moment I would rather have forgotten, 'because your mind couldn't draw a rapid enough series of relations between your snowboarding down a mountain, and a Buddhist monk you unexpectedly found standing in the path of your oncoming snowboard!

'Now consider this as an example from real life, not from theoretical life!' he declared. 'Buddhists, you see, are the ultimate realists. We like theories, but only if they have realistic applications to actual day-to-day, or lifetime-to-lifetime circumstances.

'In day-to-day life,' he said, 'you are constantly dealing with the unknown. Yes, there will be a certain amount of repetition in most people's lives. For example, you may go to school each day at approximately the same time and follow the same route.

'But one day, something may occur on your way to school that was quite unexpected, something that you could not have anticipated would ever possibly occur at precisely that moment. Perhaps a car swerves out of control and suddenly bears down on you, or perhaps the most beautiful girl you have ever seen suddenly walks past you.

'If you were thinking logically, in straight lines, at the time, you would probably not react quickly and correctly to what was happening to you during that unexpected moment. Employing the hierarchical Western system of thought, you would need to analyze, consider, and evaluate before you could act. But in real life, not in theory, by the time you had done so, you would have probably missed your chance to avoid disaster or seize an unexpected opportunity.

'The most successful people in the world are those who think relationally,' Master Fwap continued. 'Of course they can use hierarchical logical analysis too, when it is beneficial for them to do so. But most highly effective and successful people don't rely on hierarchical logical analysis for most of their problem-solving; instead they solve problems relationally with the assistance of their second attention.

'Most highly successful people live in a state of creative and happy emptiness. Unlike average people who become overly absorbed in what they are thinking about, dealing with currently, anticipating or remembering, individuals who think relationally – from the center of the circle of consciousness – can see opportunities that other people overlook, and simultaneously create rapid relations that enable them to quickly and successfully seize these opportunities and avoid disasters.

'To sum it all up in overly simplistic terms,' Master Fwap said tersely, 'success in life primarily depends on two things: timing, and a person's ability to create rapid and accurate relations within one's own mind.'

'But wait a second, Master Fwap. How does thinking relationally affect my walking past the most beautiful girl I have ever seen?'

'If you were thinking logically,' he replied with a laugh, 'you would probably not react properly or quickly enough to meet and impress her. Logically, if she was the most beautiful woman you had ever seen, you would be so overwhelmed by her beauty that you wouldn't react quickly enough, and you would miss the opportunity to introduce yourself to her.

'Or you would react logically. You might like to meet her, but remember you are on your way to school. You might not have enough time to meet her without being late to class.

'Also, how would you react?' he inquired rhetorically. 'Using logic, you could only rely on your past experiences, those that are in your current memory, to draw information from, on how to approach her. You would have to quickly think of a way to create a logical relationship between yourself and what you were going to say to her. But by the time you got all of this constructed in your mind, chances are she would be long gone!'

'But Master Fwap,' I stammered, 'I don't see how thinking relationally, or not thinking at all, or whatever it is you are trying to explain to me, would help me to meet and impress her.'

'It is easier than you realize, but you must think relationally to understand what I am talking about,' he replied with a soft chuckle.

'As I said before,' he continued, 'the mind is like an onion; it is made up of countless layers. The layers closest to the surface of your conscious awareness are the storehouse of your memories and experiences from your current lifetime. But beneath those layers are deeper layers that contain your past-life experiences, and deeper still there are layers that access the pure intelligence of the universe itself, which I refer to as the second attention.

'When you think relationally, when you have the full awareness of your mind – all of those layers are at your disposal. You can immediately draw information from your past lives or, if the information you want can't even be found there, you can draw information directly from your second attention.

'Perhaps you have had many past lives in which you knew equally beautiful women,' Master Fwap said seductively. 'You could draw information about the best way to react and speak to her from your past-life memories. And if you think relationally, via the second attention, you could access that information instantly.

'From the center of the circle, you can instantly find whatever it is you need to know,' Master Fwap explained, 'in order to react properly to any situation. Trust me, this is true!'

'Master Fwap, how can this be?'

'There are two ways of doing things in life,' Master Fwap replied. 'One way is to do things in and through structures; the other way is to do things by going outside of structures.

'Doing things in and through structures,' he continued, 'is what most people do. If you want to build a house, for example, you decide what type of house you want to build, choose a site for it, create a blueprint, and then build your house following the blueprint.

'But there is another way to build a house – the Tantric Buddhist way. You first let the site select you. Then you go there and allow the site's power to show you what type of house should be built there, and then you build it.'

'So what does that have to do with the second attention?' I was starting to get confused by Master Fwap's explanation, and I wanted him to clear up my lack of understanding before he went any further.

'Well.' Master Fwap said in a bright and happy tone, 'I suppose it has everything to do with the second attention. That's my point.'

'But Master Fwap!' I protested, 'what is the second attention?'

'The second attention is the magical side of life,' he calmly replied. 'There are two sides to existence, the side you see and the side you don't. The side that you see is the first attention, and the side you don't see is the second attention.'

Master Fwap paused, and looked at me. In the dim light of the cave I could vaguely make out enough of his facial expression to tell that he was very proud of what he had just said, even though I didn't know why.

'The second attention,' he continued, 'is beyond structures. By structures I mean the dimensions of time, space and mind. The second attention is a field of endless light that exists just beyond our grasp. It is the home of what human beings call magic and miracles.'

'I still don't understand what it is,' I complained.

'Oh yes you do,' he remarked casually. 'You use the second attention whenever you go snowboarding; that is why you are able to do it so well.

'Most people don't believe in the second attention,' he factually stated. 'They have never experienced it, even though it surrounds them and the world they live in, all of the time.

'The second attention is the power of life!' he declared. 'It exists within every atom of the universe; it is the power behind perception and all things which you perceive.

'You see, my young friend.' Master Fwap was suddenly more gentle, as if he was explaining something very complicated to a small child. 'There are many unseen miracles of life. The very existence of the universe is a miracle. The fact that we live and are aware is a miracle. The fact that we die and are reborn is a miracle.

'These things cannot be understood by the thinking and calculating portions of our mind. We can examine aspects of these miracles with those parts of our mind, but we can never truly understand them.

'The second attention is an essence,' he continued. 'It exists whether we are aware of it or not. Through the practice of short path Tantric Buddhist Yoga, we learn to become a bridge between the power of the second attention – the world of magic – and the dimensionality of the first attention, which is, of course, the day-to-day world we normally live in.

'Through meditation and other Tantric practices we learn to tap into the magical side of creation. This is the invisible side of life that underlies and supports all of the universes.

'The second attention is ancient and powerful!' he said abruptly. 'It doesn't care for our puny reason. It can do things that are unimaginable – as a matter of fact, it does them all the time! And when you allow its power to pulse through you, then you and your life become the vehicle of some of its magic.'

'So, Master Fwap, what does all of this have to do with yoga and enlightenment?'

'It is easy,' he replied. 'Normally it takes many incarnations of yogic practice for people to make major structural changes in their vibratory patterns and in the universes they have the ability to incarnate in. But when the power of the second attention is released into the practice of yoga, or anything for that matter, the miracle power of the universe enters into it, allowing things that would normally take place at a much slower pace to occur much faster. It even makes some things happen that would otherwise be totally impossible.'

'So then why doesn't everyone who practices Buddhism use the second attention?' I asked.

'They do,' he replied. 'Whenever they meditate or focus on the worlds of enlightenment and the higher dimensions inside their minds that is exactly what they are doing! But most Buddhists only touch the second attention lightly. It empowers them and gives them a better life and that is enough for them. But that is not the case for all Buddhists,' he laughed. 'Some of us want to surf the inner Himalayas, you know.'

'What do you mean by that, Master Fwap?'

'Most Buddhists, and most people for that matter, are easily satisfied and I assure you there is nothing wrong with that. But some of us are drawn to more . . . it is our karma. We want to go further into enlightenment and deeper into ecstasy; we want to merge with and become the totality of enlightenment! We want to transcend the self as soon as possible.

'So those people who want to attain enlightenment as quickly as possible practice Tantric Buddhism because Tantric Buddhism is the fastest path for attaining enlightenment; it's really that simple.'

'But what does that have to do with me surfing the Himalayas?' I inquired suspiciously.

'Let me just say,' Master Fwap replied with a mock tone of chastisement, 'that you, like a Tantric Buddhist, are a person who seeks peak experiences. Most people your age wouldn't need to leave their native country, where there are plenty of high mountains to go snowboarding on, and travel all the way to the Himalayas to snowboard. But you needed to. It is part of your karma, because you are the way that you are.'

'Is that wrong, Master Fwap? Am I being greedy?'

'No, not at all. It is simply how you work. People who seek enlightenment rapidly on the Tantric short path, as I did, and someone like yourself, who wants to snowboard the highest and most majestic mountains in the world, are not being greedy. It is simply what their karma draws them to.

'The important thing, from a yogic point of view,' he continued, 'is not to become egotistical. If a person who follows the Tantric short path to enlightenment feels "spiritually superior" to someone who is following a more gradual path to enlightenment, then that person is making a great mistake, and is missing the entire point of the practice of yoga.

'Practicing yoga,' Master Fwap continued, 'teaches us that we are all the same. We may have different external tendencies from other people we know, and we may also have different awareness levels, but inwardly we are all one.

'When you feel that you are superior to someone else, you lack compassion. Compassion is a word Buddhists use to express the realization that even though we may differ greatly in evolution, appearance, talents or intelligence from other beings in the universe, we are all equally valuable in the eyes of eternity. This is wisdom.

'When you feel superior to someone else,' he continued, 'whether it's on the pathway to enlightenment, in the sport of snowboarding, in business or in any other aspect of your life, you cut yourself off from the inner light of enlightenment. You no longer feel happy. Instead you are alone with your judgments, with your egotism, and with your limited self.

'To reach the unlimited ecstatic self within us, we must overcome all feelings of both superiority and inferiority. Feelings of inferiority are simply another manifestation of the ego in disguise.

'I'm not asking you to be falsely humble and to avoid success, or to not do the things that you enjoy.'

Master Fwap said with a hearty laugh. 'That is not the Tantric way.

'Simply realize that we all have different karmas,' he explained. 'Some people have developed aspects of themselves, specific talents and abilities in this or in other lives, in ways that others have not. See and enjoy the differences and accomplishments of others.

'Enjoy your own struggles and successes too. If you want to be happy, avoid falling into the trap of egotism about what you do and who you perceive yourself to be, and don't be threatened or feel jealous of someone else because they can do something that you can't, or because they have something that you don't.

'Remember, we are all made up equally of the intelligent light of enlightenment! That light chooses to express itself uniquely through each one of us in its own mysterious and special fashion, for reasons that cannot be known here.'

'But Master Fwap,' I asked, 'isn't there a difference between desire and doing what is right? If I just do whatever it is that I am drawn to, that won't make me happy, will it?'

'You are correct. There is certainly a difference between desire and karma,' he replied. 'Not that there's anything wrong with experiencing desires,' he continued. 'Remember desires are just another way that the universe expresses its love of itself, in and through us.

'Karma is the level of your awareness – what you are drawn toward in life,' he explained. 'It won't go away until your level of awareness changes. It is like the earth circling the sun: as long as the sun's gravitational field is stronger than the earth's, the earth has to circle the sun.

'Your awareness, which is your karma, is what hooks you to things,' Master Fwap explained. 'That is not the same as desire. Desire is a short-term pull toward an object, experience, or some other aspect of life. Desire fades with time, sometimes even in minutes or within seconds of its fulfillment. Very few desires last for more than a few years, let alone for an entire incarnation.

'So when you are inexplicably pulled toward something, an experience, or someone, and that pull won't go away, that is how you can know that it is your karma, not simply another transient desire. And if it is an especially strong pull that won't go away, then it is probably from your past lives. And if you don't follow your karma, if you try to avoid it and run away from whatever your karma happens to be, you will never be happy or at peace with yourself, no matter what you do or achieve in this or in any other world.'

'So what does all of this have to do with relational thinking, Master Fwap?'

'Your mind has the ability to perceive both relationally and logically,' he answered happily. 'Both methods of perception are good and serve different purposes. The problem is that most people are taught to perceive things in only one way – logically. They never develop their innate ability to perceive things from the center of the circle. Now do you understand?'

'I think so, Master Fwap,' I said, somewhat hesitantly.

'Good, then please give me an example,' he said with a big laugh.

I paused for a minute to collect my thoughts. Sitting in silence, while I was trying to put together everything that Master Fwap had just said I suddenly realized that I wasn't at all cold. I was just about to comment on the cave's surprising warmth, when I remembered that Master Fwap was patiently waiting for my answer to his question.

'Master Fwap, you are saying that the universe is one big mind. Am I right?'

'Exactly!' he replied.

'And all of us are part of that big mind, and it is also a part of us.'

'Yes,' he agreed,' please continue . . .'

'Well, relationally speaking, when I suspend my thoughts I go into the second attention, and in my second attention I see the universe differently, from what you refer to as the center of the circle of perception. From there I can draw from my current and past-life knowledge, or directly from the second attention, which is the essential knowing of the universe.

'So, if I was snowboarding down a mountain and a Buddhist monk suddenly appeared in front of me, instead of panicking and losing it like I did when I surfed you, I could flow with the experience. To do this I would simply accept the fact that you were there, as if it were an everyday occurrence – not freak out – and deal with it from a deeper level of awareness. Is that right?'

'You've got it!' he said and clapped his hands together in applause.

We sat in the cave for a little while longer. Master Fwap told me that I needed time for my new understanding of relational thinking to sink in before we left the cave's helpful energy.

Sitting in silence in the cave, next to Master Fwap, a variety of different sensations passed through my body and mind. At times I felt as if all the universe was part of me, and at other times I felt that I was a small part of it.

After some time, we left the cave of seeing, and

journeyed down the winding mountain trail until we reached the rhododendron forest below. After walking through the forest for about an hour, we entered a valley in which there was a small hermitage run by some Buddhist monks who were friends of Master Fwap.

We spent the next several days at the monastery with Master Fwap's monk friends, and I have never been so happy before or since. But that's another story for another chapter.

ॐ

CHAPTER FIFTEEN

Peak Experiences

ॐ

The ancient monastery was built into the side of a mountain cliff on the edge of the rhododendron forest. It housed fifteen Buddhist monks, although, Master Fwap confided to me, it had once housed more than a hundred.

It was made of stone, wood and plaster. Dozens of brightly colored prayer flags, and stones carved with 'Om Mani Padme Hum,' decorated its front courtyard. The meditation hall was large: I estimated that well over one hundred monks could simultaneously meditate there. Behind and above the meditation hall were a kitchen and study rooms.

We had arrived at sunset, just as the monastery lamps were being lit. As the two of us stood surveying the monastery, a pair of monks came out into the front courtyard and blew through two musical instruments that looked like seven-foot-long oboes. I can't say that the sounds they made were pleasing to me, but judging from the bright and happy expression on Master Fwap's face he seemed to enjoy their music.

Shortly after our arrival, all the monks came out to the courtyard to greet us. They smiled at me and several of the younger monks came over directly to me and bowed.

I observed from their attentiveness to him, that the monks who lived in the monastery seemed to know, like and have a deep respect for Master Fwap. I also noticed that he acted differently around them than he did with me. He seemed more at ease.

We were led to the kitchen, where we were seated at a long table with a number of the monks. They all laughed and chatted with Master Fwap in Nepali, while two of the younger monks served us both tea.

After tea, Master Fwap and I were conducted into the north wing and ushered into the room belonging to the head Lama of the monastery.

He was very old. He sat on a meditation couch in the large room that served as both his bedroom and office. He greeted me with a warm, broad smile.

I liked him immediately. Despite his advanced years, there was something very youthful about him; he seemed to me to be very innocent and vulnerable. Master Fwap said something to him in a different language, and then the two of them started giggling like children.

Later Master Fwap explained to me that the head Lama, like himself, was Tibetan. They had been conversing and making jokes about me in their native language, so that only the two of them would understand!

After a few minutes, one of the younger monks appeared noiselessly at the head Lama's door, and conducted me to a different section of the monastery, where I would be staying.

ॐ

I was given a small room to stay in at the end of the south wing. It was sparsely furnished and smelled perpetually of incense.

In the center of the room was a cot. Built into one of the room's walls were two small chests of drawers made of a dark wood that resembled teak. In the front of the room, opposite the entryway door, hung a brightly colored tanka, depicting scenes from the life of the Buddha.

I don't remember dreaming during the nights I slept in the monastery. My days were spent taking walks with the younger monks and helping around the kitchen.

One of the younger monks who was about my age had undertaken the task of teaching me Nepali. In return, he asked me to teach him English. He and I spent our mornings and afternoons together, when I wasn't working in the kitchen, walking around the monastery grounds pointing at anything we could find to teach each other words in Nepali and in English.

His name was Ananda. In the little English that he spoke, he told me he was born in southwestern Nepal in a small village. He told me that he had lived in several other monasteries before coming here. He referred to the monastery we were in as the 'cliff monastery.' He said he was seventeen years old.

I liked the routine of the monastery. Every morning we would get up with the sun. We bathed in a freezing cold waterfall that came roaring down the mountainside, and then after returning to the kitchen for hot buttered tea, we all would go to the meditation hall for morning meditation.

The meditation hall was windowless. It was lit with dozens of small candles. The walls were covered with brightly colored tankas that depicted Buddhas, gods, goddesses and otherwordly scenes in fantastically complicated paintings.

Each morning I would sit next to Master Fwap, facing the front of the hall in a cross-legged position, on a meditation cushion. At the front of the room, next to a statue of the Buddha, the head Lama stood motionless until all of the other monks were present and seated. Then he would ring a small bell. Immediately everyone would close their eyes and enter into meditation.

Trying to follow Master Fwap's instructions, I meditated as best I could. At the beginning of each session, I mostly thought. But partway through the morning meditation my thoughts would begin to slow, and occasionally – for very short periods of time – they would completely stop.

During these times I felt similar to the way that I had when I had been sitting next to Master Fwap in the cave of seeing. I could feel a perfect stillness within me. The universe seemed to melt into me and I into it; I felt like I was a part of everything and I had no fear.

I noticed that each morning, about fifteen minutes after the meditation session had ended, everything became very shiny. My physical vision seemed to clear and everything I saw became brighter and more precise. One morning after meditation, I asked Master Fwap about this phenomenon. He told me that things were always this bright, but that I needed my morning meditation to clear my mind enough to see just how beautiful life really was.

ॐ

Samadhi is the Top of the Mountain

One day, after we had been staying at the cliff monastery for about a week, Master Fwap and I spent an afternoon in the monastery garden. It was a sunny day and I felt lazy and warm sitting in the garden with a cup of steaming buttered tea in my hand.

Master Fwap was all smiles that day. He told me we would have to leave in a few days, and that I should enjoy the time we had left at the monastery. He remarked that this particular monastery was his favorite in all of the Himalayas. He said that he came here whenever he needed to clear his mind and rejuvenate his spirit.

'Normally when I come here,' he began. 'I spend most of my time meditating in this garden. The luminous energy lines of this particular valley all converge right here in this garden. These energy lines are particularly conducive to samadhi.'

'Why is that?' I inquired.

'Because they emanate from a dimension of perfect light!' he replied with a bright and happy laugh. 'As I told you in the cave of seeing, different physical locations are hooked to different dimensions. Buddhist monasteries are built on locations that interphase with dimensions that are of the brightest and most perfect light,' he replied.

'Look around you,' he continued. 'We are in a valley that is surrounded by the Himalayas on all sides. There is nothing else here except snow-covered mountains, and the rhododendron forest. The only people who live here are Buddhist monks who constantly meditate on the dharma – on the happiest thoughts and feelings in the universe. There is no selfishness here. All the energies of the monks are directed toward merging their minds with the ocean of pure nirvanic enlightenment.'

'But Master Fwap, is all of the higher energy here

because of the luminous energy lines, or is the high energy here emanating from the meditating monks?'

'Originally there were no monks and there was no monastery here,' he responded. 'There were only the Himalayas and the rhododendron forest. The dimensional planes that correspond to this valley we are in were then, and still are, made up of pure intelligent light.

'The Himalayas are filled with places like this,' he continued. 'And since there are few, if any, people around these locations, these places of power and enlightenment have remained relatively unpolluted by the aura of worldly human beings.'

'Master Fwap, are there other places like this outside of the Himalayas?'

'Yes, there are quite a few on each continent, and also on some islands,' he replied with a smile. 'But most of them have become so polluted by the cities that have been built near or on them that they cannot be used for achieving samadhi any more.'

'Why do you need a special place to experience samadhi?' I asked. 'I thought that if you were enlightened you could go into samadhi in any location. If samadhi is a deep meditative state of mind, what does physical location have to do with achieving it?'

Master Fwap laughed delightedly at my question. I could tell he was amused by the fact that I had finally decided to ask him something about meditation, instead of my perpetual topic, snowboarding.

'There are really two issues involved here.' Master Fwap began, 'and I want you to see them as complementary, not as being opposed or unrelated to each other. They are both equally important.

'The first issue is understanding what the samadhis are, and how they are attained: this is purely a technical understanding of meditation techniques and methods. The second issue is how the higher energies of parallel dimensions and power spots can be used to heighten overall spiritual awareness, and how they can make it easier for a person to experience the samadhis.'

'Master Fwap, I thought you said that samadhi was the absence of thought? I've experienced that several times since we've been here, during my morning meditations. Does that mean I have been entering into samadhi already?'

Master Fwap laughed heartily! His eyes twinkled with delight as he said: 'No, I'm afraid that what you have experienced so far, in your early morning meditations, is a few good minutes of meditation, but not samadhi.'

'Well, how can you tell what samadhi is?' I asked, frustrated.

'Samadhi,' Master Fwap replied, 'is, of course, the absence of thought. Let us say that the absence of thought is one of the indications that you have entered into a deep state of meditation. But there are several other aspects to the experience of samadhi that must also be present, if what you are experiencing is really samadhi.

'Let me begin by saying that the experience in meditation of samadhi is not a great achievement. In this world it is, however, a very rare achievement. Of all of the hundreds of thousands of Buddhist monks who meditate every day, only a handful of them are able to experience samadhi every time they meditate.

'According to our yogic traditions, samadhi means complete awareness of God, or to put it in less religious terms, samadhi means that your mind and the mind of the universe are, for a time, merged in an absolute ecstatic union.

'There are said to be three stages of samadhi –

189

Salvikalpa samadhi, Nirvikalpa samadhi, and Sahaja samadhi. Salvikalpa samadhi is like accidentally falling into a beautiful and pure lake of absolute bliss. You did not fall in intentionally, but you found it refreshing nevertheless.

'Nirvikalpa samadhi is like intentionally diving into the same lake and swimming and playing in it for a time. Sahaja samadhi is like living on a houseboat in the middle of the lake of bliss, and occasionally coming ashore for supplies.

'The mind of infinity is everywhere!' Master Fwap shouted in a jubilant outburst. 'It is all around us, inside of us, and beyond us: it is everywhere and nowhere at the same time.

'To an extent, we experience the mind of God in all things. We experience it in the world that we see and feel every day, the people we know, the thoughts we think and in the emotions that we feel. The physical universes, astral dimensions and causal dimensions are simply different aspects of the mind of God.

'But when we experience life through our senses and with our thoughts, we don't experience its essential nature, its most pure and radiant form. Instead we only experience the external veneer of life's ecstasy.

'Most of the water in a lake lies hidden beneath its surface,' Master Fwap continued. 'In much the same way, only a small portion of life can be seen. The vast majority of life is nonphysical; it exists beyond the physical surface of life, in other dimensions.

'If you want to experience life in its totality, it is necessary to enter into samadhi. Stopping your thoughts for a few minutes during meditation – which you have experienced several times in the meditation hall over the past few mornings – will give you a glimpse of the inner depths of infinity. But in samadhi, you gain more than a glimpse, you will experience the infinite, eternal and perfect depths of existence.

'The experience of samadhi is never the same twice,' he continued. 'In some ways it is like climbing one of our Himalayan mountains. The weather conditions around a Himalayan mountain, and the amount of snow covering it, are constantly changing. Even though you may climb the same mountain again and again, you will never have exactly the same experience twice, because of the mountain's ever-changing climatic conditions.

'Because nirvana is endless, ever-new, changeless yet ever-changing, and since your ability to experience it – to climb higher up the mountain of meditation, so to speak – also increases as your life becomes more fluid and powerful, your experiences in samadhi – your ecstatic journeys into nirvana – are never exactly the same.

'Samadhi is ecstasy beyond comprehension,' Master Fwap continued. 'During deep meditation, as you start to enter into samadhi, at first every cell in your body will be filled with a fiery ecstasy. This ecstasy starts at the base of your spine, and rises as the kundalini energy ascends up your sushumna.

'Your sushumna is the primary conduit of the kundalini energy in your nonphysical body. It is an astral nerve tube that runs between and connects all of your major chakras. It begins at the base of your spine, where your first chakra is located, and then runs up through your spleen chakra, navel chakra, heart chakra, throat chakra and ends in your sixth chakra, the third eye, which is located in the center of your forehead. It runs in the astral plane next to and along your spinal column.

'To go into samadhi you must pull the kundalini energy up from your root chakra, the first chakra at the base of your spine, all the way up to your third eye! Then you must move all the kundalini energy you have amassed at your sixth chakra, the third eye, up and into your seventh chakra – which we in Buddhist Yoga refer to as the crown chakra.

'This is the difficult part, because the crown chakra is not directly connected to the third eye by the sushumna. It takes a great deal of willpower, and total vibratory purity, to move the kundalini energy all of the way up to the crown chakra from your third eye.

'When the kundalini energy enters your crown chakra, you experience samadhi. As I mentioned before, samadhi is the direct experience of nirvana.

'The crown chakra is the nexus of one thousand dimensional planes. That is why, in Buddhist Yoga, it is often referred to as the thousand-petaled lotus of light.

'The amount of kundalini you are able to bring into your crown chakra,' Master Fwap said, 'will determine how many of those dimensions – the petals of the crown chakra – become simultaneously active. The different samadhis are simply measurements of how many of the thousand petals of the crown chakra you are able to simultaneously access. The more dimensions in your crown chakra you can simultaneously access, the more ecstatic your samadhi is, and the more complete your experience of nirvana will be.

'Please remember,' Master Fwap said in a strong and formal tone, 'that what I have just described to you is only a verbal blueprint of how the experience of samadhi is achieved. It is, at best, a flow chart of how the kundalini moves.

'There is much, much more to achieving samadhi, enlightenment, and experiencing nirvana than I have expressed to you in this simple verbal description! You learn the subtleties of the samadhis, and how to become enlightened and merge with nirvana, from being personally initiated by, and directly studying with an enlightened Buddhist master.'

'Master Fwap, how does the movement of all of that energy through your chakras affect you?'

'As the kundalini energy moves up your sushumna and passes through your chakras – which it does when you are capable of stopping all your thoughts for protracted periods of time – it burns away all the impurities that exist within your physical body, your mind and your subtle body. When all of those impurities have been completely burned away, your mind turns into pure light.

'Then, as light,' Master Fwap continued, 'the essence of your spirit body perfectly enters nirvana. At first there is a slight sense of differentiation. It is like slipping your feet into a pair of shoes that fit perfectly; you can feel your feet slipping into them for a moment, but then, after a few minutes, you don't feel that your shoes are separate from your feet anymore.

'After going into samadhi for many lifetimes,' Master Fwap explained, 'there is no sense of individuality. You are absorbed into the heart of light without motion. You rest there unknowingly. All awareness of this, or of any other plane or world, comes to an end. There is only light, the pure and perfect awareness of nirvana.

'Both the depth of your entrance into nirvana, and the amount of time you spend in that perfect absorption, will depend upon the strength of your mind, body and spirit, the amount of energy you have at your disposal, and also, to a certain degree, upon your physical location.'

'Why is that, Master Fwap?'

'All places are not the same! They may look similar to the unenlightened eye, but they are connected to different dimensions, and possess different levels and types of pranic energy.

'One of the tricks to entering into samadhi,' Master Fwap continued, 'after you have experienced the proper training and learned the secret techniques from an enlightened master, is to be in the right place at the right time.'

'Master Fwap,' I asked, 'what do you mean by training, and what are the secret techniques?'

He laughed heartily in response to my question. 'You do want to know everything all at once,' he smiled. 'I suppose that is the American way.

'Well,' he continued, 'you can't expect to experience samadhi without the proper training, can you? Entering into samadhi is a little like flying an airplane. Without any instruction at all, you probably won't know how to start the plane. With a little instruction, you may be able to take off, but you won't know how to fly. With a fair amount of instruction you will be able to fly in normal situations. If you want to fly at higher altitudes, where the weather is more problematic but the view is also more breathtaking, you will need a great deal of instruction.'

'But Master Fwap, I thought you said that a person simply had to raise the kundalini energy up their spine and get it to light up their crown chakra? Why would anyone need instruction beyond the techniques necessary to do that?'

'Once again, please be patient. I know that my explanations are, at times, quite long. But you are learning a very complicated subject, Buddhist Yoga, and it is essential that you grasp the fundamentals before we venture out together into interdimensional space.

'Having an enlightened master,' he continued, 'is an absolute necessity for the serious student of Buddhist Yoga.'

'Why, Master Fwap? I'm sure it makes it easier and

faster to learn any subject if you have a good teacher, but why can't you just learn Buddhist Yoga from a book, the way you can any other subject?'

'Buddhist Yoga is the study of power, balance, and knowledge,' Master Fwap responded. 'These three steps lead to enlightened awareness. None of them can be skipped, or you will fail to enter into samadhi.

'A certain amount of the basic teachings of Buddhist Yoga can be learned from a book,' he said with a concerned smile. 'For example, you can read about the types of things that you and I discuss together. But in order to really practice higher yoga, you need the energy, vibrational purity, example, humor, patience and wisdom of a living master.

'The first and most basic thing you gain from studying with a master is pure power,' Master Fwap explained. 'When you are with your master, he transfers high-grade kundalini energy into your subtle body.

'The empowerments from your master energize and activate your chakras, allowing you to do things that you could not possibly do with the amount of energy you normally have at your disposal.

'Think of it this way,' he continued. 'If you are a student at college, and you have very little money in your checking account, the scope of your activities will be limited. But if you have a scholarship and you get money deposited into your checking account on a regular basis, then you will be able to do much more.

'Your master's auric empowerment awakens your past-life abilities and talents, and can even boost your IQ.

'When you study directly with an enlightened master,' he continued to explain, 'you also gain vibrational purity. Just being in your master's aura on a regular basis will detoxify your aura, and even help you to remove many of the negative karmic patterns that you have acquired over the course of your incarnations.

'Another important thing you gain by studying with a master is example. By watching your master in different situations, you will get to personally see how a Buddhist master displays grace under pressure, in all situations. Life is never easy, not even for the enlightened. As a matter of fact, enlightened masters are often persecuted by the society they live in.'

'Why is that, Master Fwap?'

'An enlightened master is cuttingly honest with people. Human beings are so used to lying to each other, and to themselves, that they have come to call a great deal of their lying the truth. But enlightened masters always tell the real truth. This tends to make them unpopular with lots of people, including their own students.

'But if what you really seek is enlightenment,' Master Fwap continued in a strong and emphatic tone of voice, 'then you will want and need your master's honesty, even if it bruises your big ego on a regular basis.'

'So what does all of this have to do with going into samadhi, and how physical locations like this valley can enhance that?' I inquired.

'It is because of the pranic currents here,' he replied coyly.

'Exactly what is a pranic current?' I asked, in a frustrated tone of voice.

'It is the invisible current of energy that flows from one dimension to another. If the pranic current is highly charged, which occurs when the energy comes from a dimension that vibrates very rapidly, then the physical area where that dimension crosses over becomes highly charged too. The valley we are in is such a place.

'If the pranic currents come from a dimension that

vibrates more slowly than the energy in our own dimension, then the physical area of pranic crossover becomes negatively charged.'

'What does that do?'

'If you spend time in such a place, it will slow down the vibratory rate of your subtle body. You will feel tired and drained. If you stay there too long you can become physically sick. In addition, being in a negatively charged area will make it difficult, if not impossible, for you to perceive things psychically.

'On the other hand, a valley such as the one we are in right now is filled with positive pranic energy: this energy speeds up the vibratory rate of your subtle body. When you enter into meditation here, whether it is a basic level of meditation or samadhi, the added boost that you receive from the positively charged prana that is available in this location will make it much easier for you to achieve a higher state of meditation.

'When the wind moves in the same direction that an airplane does, it significantly speeds up the airplane,' Master Fwap stated factually. 'If the airplane flies against the wind, it slows down. Pranic currents act in much the same way: they can assist you in your meditation practice, or make it more difficult, according to the type and intensity of the pranic energy present.

'That's enough talking for now,' he said with a gentle laugh. 'Let us meditate here for awhile and then go and find the Lama.'

Master Fwap closed his eyes and entered into meditation. In a few moments he was surrounded by golden light. After a few more minutes, the golden light emanating from him became so thick that I could hardly see him even though we were sitting outdoors and it was broad daylight!

After watching the golden light flow around Master

Fwap for several minutes, I closed my eyes and let my mind relax. The next thing I knew, Master Fwap was tapping me on the shoulder. I opened my eyes and, much to my surprise, it was almost dark. I had been sitting in meditation for several hours, even though it had only seemed like seconds to me.

Master Fwap was definitely right. The higher pranic currents in the valley made it much easier for me to meditate.

Master Fwap stood up and stretched. Then the two of us started walking in silence back to the monastery. The only noise that could be heard in the valley was the sound of our feet echoing against the ancient courtyard steps.

LAST CHAPTER

The Emptiness of Snow

ॐ

Master Fwap and I spent several more days staying at the cliff monastery. During that time I had the chance to practice meditation and learn more Nepali. Toward the end of our stay, I began to feel restless. Master Fwap told me that the pranic currents in the valley were a little too strong for me, and that was why I was feeling the way I was.

We left the monastery and followed a trail that took us through a series of valleys between several large snow-covered mountain ranges. It seemed strange to be hiking through green fields and forests, when we were always surrounded on both sides by steep, snow-covered mountains.

We passed through several small villages along our route. Master Fwap seemed to be friends with everyone who lived in Nepal! Wherever we went we were treated as honored guests. We were given food and buttered tea by the villagers without having to ask, and many of the villagers politely inquired if the board that I was carrying on my back was a religious object.

On the fifth day of our journey, we ascended a high mountain pass. We spent the better part of the morning hiking straight up. When we reached the summit of the mountain, we sat down to rest on the snow and ice-covered ground. As usual, I was soaked with perspiration from our climb, and Master Fwap didn't seem to have perspired at all.

We sat in silence for a few minutes. Gradually the pounding in my chest subsided and my breathing evened out. I turned to look at Master Fwap, and I saw that he had closed his eyes and was absorbed in meditation.

I looked down at the scenery below me. The green valleys and snow-covered mountains of Nepal seemed to stretch out into forever. The world was silent and beautiful. Unlike the stressed-out world that I came from, this world had no sound of cars, no smog, no other signs of man's 'progress.' The world that met my eyes here was uncorrupted and naturally pure.

'You see, this is life,' Master Fwap began. 'It is empty and pure, like the snow on the Himalayas.'

I turned and saw that Master Fwap had opened his eyes and was looking out at the same scene I had been absorbed in just moments before.

'But Master Fwap, how can you say life is empty and pure like snow? The world man has created is a horrible place. It is filled with noise and pollution. This is one of the few clean places left on the earth. And that's not the half of it. People are cruel to each other. They kill each other in wars, steal from each other, and oppress each other in a thousand different ways! How can you say the world is empty and pure? I think it is the opposite: it is crowded and impure.'

'Yes,' he replied, 'to the outward eye it might seem that way. But first you must understand the emptiness and purity of our Himalayan snow; then perhaps you will see why I believe that the world is empty and pure too.'

'Master Fwap, I don't understand what you mean.'

'The Himalayan snow is empty and pure. By that I mean that it comes from the sky, covers the mountains, and then melts in the warmth of sunlight. The snow here can be so thick when it falls that you cannot see one foot in front of your face. It changes the mountains. It turns them from the color of stone to pure white.'

'So what does that have to do with the world being empty and pure?' I asked.

'The world is empty and pure,' he gently replied. 'It has always been that way, and it will be so, for all of time. That cannot be changed by any of us.'

'Master Fwap, I still don't think I understand what you mean by emptiness.'

'Emptiness,' he replied, 'is a word that implies absence. I could also use the words fullness beyond comprehension. They would mean the same thing. These are the only words that I know in your language that I can use to try to express what emptiness is.'

'But Master Fwap, emptiness and fullness are opposites. How can they mean the same thing?'

'There are two worlds in front of us at all times,' Master Fwap patiently explained. 'One world everyone can see, and the other one is invisible to everyone except the enlightened.

'The world that everyone can see appears to be very solid, but in actuality it is not! The world we cannot see appears to have no reality to it at all, but in actuality it is much more solid and real than the world we see before us every day.

'The visible world we call life, and the invisible world is death,' Master Fwap continued. 'Perhaps death is not its only condition, but I cannot think of a better word.

'The apparent solidity of the visible world is ephemeral,' he remarked casually. 'Nothing lasts here. All the works of man end every second. They have absolutely no substance to them at all.'

'Master Fwap how can that be? The world exists forever; how can it end every second?'

'I will show you. The moment that we are in right now exists . . . now it has passed and we are in a new moment . . . now that moment has passed and we are in yet another moment.

'When each moment ends,' he continued, 'the world ends with it. In each new moment, the world is created again. These momentary endings and creations are what you call life. Your mind and your body experience them continuously without your realizing it.

'All of the things that happen in a moment, end in a moment. Who knows why? It is just that way. Human beings fool themselves into thinking there is a past and a future, and that things last and matter. But it is an illusion of perception.

'Nothing lasts and nothing really matters,' he said. 'Things just seem to last and matter when you experience life through your senses, and through the perceptions of your physical mind.

'This is what I mean by emptiness – the world you see all around you lacks any kind of solidity. From moment to moment it comes and goes. Why allow yourself to be bothered by anything transient that occurs here?

'I know you mean well,' Master Fwap said with a lighthearted laugh, 'and that your heart is pure. This is why karma selected you to be my disciple. You were born with a pure heart – that is to say with a pure aura. You have a pure aura because you meditated in so many of your past incarnations, and in that process you eliminated all of the impurities from your inner being.

'But wisdom tells us that our concerns – the things in life that upset us – are unreal. They only appear to matter when we don't see life as the enlightened do.'

'How do the enlightened see life, Master Fwap?'

'You were enlightened in many of your past lives – you should know,' he replied cuttingly.

'Well if I was, I certainly don't remember it. Would you please tell me how all of this looks to a person who is enlightened?'

'We are all made up of vibrating particles of intelligent light,' he replied. 'That, however, is only one side of our nature. We have another side; it is the side that only the enlightened can see.

'The emptiness of snow is death,' Master Fwap said as he made a sweeping gesture with his hand that took in everything that we could see in the vast panorama before us. 'It is the other side of all of this, what you call life.'

'What is death, Master Fwap?'

'Why, dear boy, death is life.'

'Then I suppose that life is death?' I asked hesitantly.

'Yes, exactly. Now you have it! Very good!' And so saying, Master Fwap gave me a beaming smile.

'Great, Master Fwap, but what does it mean?'

'Why, it means that the world is perfect. Nothing and no one can change it at all. The invisible world that only the enlightened can see is essence – it is eternal life. That is what we return to when we die. We go back into perfect eternal light for awhile, and then we reincarnate.

'This world that you see before you is reborn and dies every moment. When it is born it comes out of the invisible world – the world that you cannot see. When it dies it returns to that world too. That world is perfect consciousness. It is ecstasy. There is no suffering there, and there is no sense of loss, gain or pain.

'To suffer because of anything you see, feel or experience here in the world of moment to moment is a mistake! It is like becoming upset over a frightening dream. Dreams are insubstantial; they don't last. When you wake up, no matter how vivid your dream was, it is past. It no longer exists, so why allow yourself to be upset over something that no longer exists?

'When you can see the other side of life, the world you refer to as death – the mysterious undiscovered universe that lies just beyond our mind and senses – all of the pain and frustration of your life will go away. You will see that everything and everyone you love, who may appear to have been destroyed, is still just fine. They have simply moved from the world of moment to moment, back into the world of emptiness. They have returned to the reservoir of life that we call nirvana.

'The world is empty,' Master Fwap almost whispered. 'All of the people and places, the earth, the seas, mountains, deserts, forests and cities, and the beings that inhabit them, are unchangeable.

'They appear to change, oh yes!' he suddenly said loudly. 'But one part of them returns to nirvana and another part of them comes forward. You cannot see it, so it is like a magicians trick. We are convinced that something has occurred when in reality nothing has happened at all.'

'Master Fwap, how can this be?'

'It is the perfection of life,' he responded with a broad smile. 'Let me give you an example. Then perhaps you will understand why I am not sad, as you are, about what has happened to the earth.

'Consider children who are born into this world. They pass through many stages. They become adolescents, young adults, they enter into middle age, and then into old age. Then they die. Now it would appear, looking just at the surface of life, that they have gone through many changes, and then disappeared. But this is not the entire picture at all.

'On the other side of this life there are endless dimensions – endless realities that stretch on into infinity. There are worlds of form and dimensionality that are similar to our own. There are also formless worlds that are made up of pure and perfect light. Beyond both the formless and the form worlds, there is something else, nirvana, the endless and perfect source of all. Nirvana is where all of these endless worlds of formlessness and form come from.'

'But Master Fwap, how can this be? Are you saying that everything that exists now existed in nirvana before it came here?'

'Exactly! Everything is forever. There is no beginning and ending to life. There is no middle either. Things appear in this world for a short time. They have come here from nirvana. They exist here for a short time, and then they return to nirvana.

'Nirvana is emptiness,' he continued. 'It contains everything that has ever been, is now, or ever will be.'

'Does that mean that nirvana is heaven, Master Fwap?'

'Not in the way that you mean,' he replied.

'Well, if it is not heaven, what is it?'

'Think of nirvana as an endless ocean of ultimately intelligent light,' he replied. 'It stretches on forever, in all directions and throughout all times. It holds within itself, in seed form, all that can ever be.

'From time to time, manifest parts of nirvana appear here, in what we call the world. Then, after some time, these things dissolve back into essence, into their nirvanic formlessness.

'Nothing can die, and nothing can be reborn. Things only change their outer appearance. When you can see within things and people, you discover that their essence is changeless, perfect light. We are all nirvana: that which is our essential form, is the essential formlessness of perfect existence.'

ॐ

Master Fwap became silent. We sat for awhile without speaking, listening to the sound of the wind rushing through the snowy mountain passes. Then Master Fwap told me to go ahead and snowboard down the mountain. He said that I shouldn't think about what he had just said right now, but that I should reflect upon it in the future.

'Just concentrate on being the board,' he said with a laugh.

I mounted my board and shot down the mountain through the deep powder. I effortlessly cut in and out to avoid several boulders, and finished my run in record time. Master Fwap was waiting for me at the bottom of the mountain, his ochre-colored monk's robe fluttering in the breeze.

After getting off my board I walked over to Master Fwap. It had gotten quite dark, and the cold Himalayan wind made me shiver.

'You have done quite well!' he congratulated me. 'You can continue to study Buddhist Yoga with me, if you like.'

He smiled. We stood looking at each other in silence for several minutes. It was only at that moment that I realized how much I had come to love this aged and mysterious monk.

Overwhelmed with emotion, I turned my gaze away.

Then, together, Master Fwap and I descended the remainder of the snow-covered slope to the rock and gravel road that lay below us, where the two of us hitched a ride on a yellow and black tourist bus, back into Katmandu.

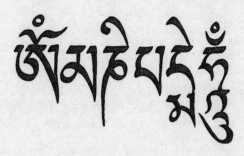